TOMBOLA

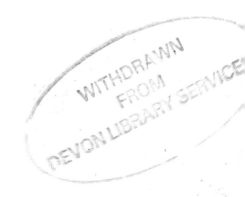

TOMBOLA

Rorie Smith

FrontList Books

Published by FrontList Books.
An imprint of Soft Editions Ltd,
Gullane, East Lothian, Scotland.

A catalogue record for this book is available from the
British Library.

ISBN: 1-84350-100-7

ISBN 13: 9781843501008

For Pin and Pegs, Nui and Bun, Dad and Alison.
With all my love.

And in memory of Mum

As soon as I got in the door I knew it was bad news.
–Pushing up roses soon, eh doc?–
He was holding up my X-rays to the light. He turned toward me, his little piggy eyes flashing.
–It's no laughing matter Mr Polianski. You're a very sick man.–
I could see he was a case who enjoyed his work. I held his gaze, not wanting to show fear.
–How long have I got then doc?–
–Two years at the outside.–
I thought for a moment and then said –That'll do nicely,– and got up and walked out.

* * *

I sat with the smokers in the rose garden at the back of the hospital and contemplated my suddenly truncated future.
I had half settled on a Caribbean cruise, slipping over the side when the pain got too much, when a sliver of cloud cut into the sun's light making me shiver.
By the time I got home I was ready for dinner. Bangkok Rose had laid my place with care. The phone was alongside the fork and the TV remote was next to the knife. On my plate, by the menu from the Chinese takeaway, was a note which read:

GON OUT. HONG KONG JIMMY GOT YOUR DINNER.

I didn't mind. Everyone deserves a night out. I studied the menu, then picked up the phone and ordered.
As I ate I thought about the doctor with the piggy eyes. I saw him at the dinner table with his wife.

–I told a man he was dying this afternoon.–
–Really dear. How interesting. Do pass the mustard.–

* * *

The next bit of bad news came a week later when I was down at the *Albert Arms* with Frank and Nell.

The door opened and Ron, the Commercial Director at Athletic Football Club, walked in.

–Well, well, look who's here,– I said to Frank.

Ron wasn't supposed to be seen with us. We were the enemy, i.e. in the way of the directors trying to wreck the club.

Frank got him a drink and he sat down.

–I just came to warn you.–

He looked around as if someone from the board might be hiding in a corner.

–I've seen some documents. They're trying to sell the club.–

–Not again,– groaned Nell.

We'd beaten off other attempts to buy us out. The problem was that the ground was worth more for housing or factories than it ever was as a football club.

–Who is it this time?– Frank asked.

Ron shook his head. –Can't tell you. Don't know. Yet. But it's serious. The chairman's told his secretary he's buying a villa in Spain and they were drinking champagne in the boardroom this morning.–

Nell said she'd go down to the council offices in the morning to see what she could find out from the planning department.

Ron looked worried. –Don't say you got anything from me.–

After that we yakked round the subject for a bit until I felt a burst of pain in my stomach and said I had to go home.

* * *

Next day Nell came round.

–I've been down to the council offices,– she said. –They're having meetings all day. It's all top secret, hush hush.–

Before we got any further Frank phoned. He'd just had the word from Ron.

–It's bad news Arthur.–

–Who's shafting us now, Frank?–

–It's bad news Arthur.–

–You've said that already!–

–You're not going to believe it Arthur.–

–Jesus, Frank who is it?–

–Worse than that.–

–Than what?–

–Jesus.–

I thought for a moment.

–Well who's that then? God?–

–Worse than God.–

After that there was only one other name, and we both said it at the same time.

–BILLY!–

Billy Petersen owned *Tombola,* one of the biggest papers in the country. Everyone knew Billy. The silver hair, the nose, the fat cat look. You couldn't open a paper or a magazine or turn on the TV without seeing his picture. Billy had lived off the fat of the land for years. People reckoned he was more powerful than the Prime Minister.

I had a fleeting hope that he was going to pour millions into the club and take us into Europe.

Then Frank said –He's going to rip the ground down Arthur. Flatten it. He wants to build a new printing plant for *Tombola.*–

–You can't fight Billy,– I heard myself say, my voice

sounding as if it were coming from outer space. I put the phone down. How many millions had the nutballs who ran our club sold us out for? How many villas in Spain had they made down-payments on? How many yachts and helicopters and pieces of skirt were they going to purchase with our life-blood?

We met the following evening at the *Albert Arms*. We were a gang of pals who had been together for years. Our common bond was our love of Athletic.

There was Frank, the best centre forward ever to play for Athletic, and Nancy, his wife.

There was Nell, who had been my best friend at school and who worked at the bookies.

There was Smithy the Traveller, who was always off on adventures, and finally there was Stan the Owl who was Nell's uncle and who owned the bookies.

We yakked around the subject for an hour, but in the end the only positive contribution came from Smithy the Traveller who said we should fire-bomb the nutjob.

I told Rose when I got home. Even she knew who Billy was.

–I'm sorry Arthur,– she said, and hugged me.

I woke up in the middle of the night feeling my guts beginning to wretch. The doctor had said that would happen, that there would be increasingly regular periods of sickness as the illness advanced.

I knelt with my head down the toilet bowl. Finally, when I had emptied my stomach, I got back up to wash my face in the basin. As I leaned forward to turn off the tap it came to me. A sudden revelation. I stood and looked at my face in the mirror and said firmly out loud

–If I'm going, I'm taking that fucker with me.–

* * *

The decision to kill Billy and the news from the piggy-eyed doctor tipped me over the edge.

Rose said I should see a psychiatrist. She said –You keep on like that they're going to lock you up.–

But I couldn't help myself. There was no doubt I was an obsessive. I always took extreme positions.

Yesterday Rose had said –This week so far we have had Stephen Hawking, Tony Blair, the Tour de France, and world poverty and it's still only chuffing Tuesday!–

But I could feel myself bubbling over.

I went shopping in *Krap U Luv* and felt disgusted.

I saw a woman standing by the meat counter and went up to her and said –Don't worry love, they've just sent for some more kangaroo legs from Australia.–

The next minute I was in the manager's office opposite a leery looking beef in a suit.

–What's your problem sunshine, your knob not working properly or what?–

I wasn't afraid of him so I said –My problem is that you're selling thirty seven different types of dog food to people who are too fat to waddle out of your store. At the same time there are people in Africa living on grass. That's my problem, and if you had brains between your ears instead of pork scratchings it'd be your problem too.–

The next minute the beefy security guard was evicting me.

–They'll get you too,– I yelled back at him, my face up against the glass door. –The Africans and the Chinese will gobble you all up for dinner!–

In the car park I spotted a woman loading a dozen grocery bags into the back of a car the size of a truck.

I went up to her and tapped her on the shoulder.

–You know that you could feed an African family for a month with that lot?–

–You what?– She turned to stare at me. Then she yelled –Victor!–

The next moment a big brute of a bloke had me up against the side of the truck and was pummelling my head against the door.

Eventually the woman shouted –Leave him go Victor, he's a waste of space. I've seen him here before.–

* * *

A week later *Krap U Luv* sent me a letter saying I was banned from every *Krap U Luv* store in the country in perpetuity and for ever, legal, legal, harrumph, harrumph.

I put the letter in a frame and hung it carefully above the kitchen table.

A week after that I was looking at the letter framed on the wall when Rose came in and dumped a load of shopping on the table.

–What's up,– she said. –You look like a dog who's had a trip to the vet.–

There were times when you could laugh at the things Rose said. But this time I turned on her and said –You wouldn't feel so good either if the doctor said you were dying.–

After that we had a week of hysterics and crying and in the end I had to remind Rose that it was me that was dying and not her.

When I told Frank he put his arm around me and said I was the best pal he'd ever had, and I said he was the best pal I'd ever had too.

Then I told Nell and she gave me a hug and didn't say anything when I put my hands on her bum and felt her big bazookas pressing into me.

After that she went on the internet and in a week she was an expert on whatever it was I had.

She prodded and poked until in the end Rose was starting to get suspicious, so I said –You should have been a doctor, Nell, not a bookies clerk.–

–I'm just trying to help Arthur,– she said, –that's all.–
I could see she was hurt.

Smithy the Traveller said he didn't believe in doctors. He told us –There's a man in Peru who'll stick a thorn up your arse. That'll cure you!–

Thanks Smithy!

* * *

Being obsessive has made me angry.

Angry because I'm going to die and I don't want to die.

Angry because Billy Petersen has gutted our football club.

Angry because Bangkok Rose's Mum had to pick rubbish off a tip in Thailand to survive when she was a girl.

Angry because every time I go to *Krap U Luv* I see useless women who can barely write their names overloading shopping trolleys with useless crap they don't need.

Angry because White Coats like Stephen Hawking and Albert Einstein think they know everything when in cosmic terms they can barely tie their own shoe laces.

Angry because no one told Van Gogh his pictures were magic until he was dead.

Angry because General Blair is so busy bombing Iraq he hasn't got time to save the Africans.

No doubt about it, I'm on the side of the dispossessed and the poor and the people who don't know everything.

When the *QuikSnooze* planes land at Gatwick and Luton and Heathrow and Stansted, and the poor Africans who are not so poor they can't sell a cow and buy a *QuikSnooze* ticket pour out and flow like a black tide to the nearest *Krap U Luv* store and start the biggest bonfire you've ever seen with all the useless crap, then I'm going to be there cheering them on even if I do get steam rollered over in the process.

* * *

I've done all the jobs at Athletic.

I've sold tickets on the gate, handed out programmes and dished up pies and teas at half time. I've swept the stands and I've worked behind the counter in the shop.

But what I like the most is being out on the pitch. When I marked out the lines before the games or forked over the divots at half time I was a happy man.

And how many times have I stood in the centre circle and wished I could strike a ball like Frank!

There were times when we were in the League that we got gates of ten thousand, and did they roar when Frank scored and turned to face them, his hand in the air like a Roman Emperor!

We've also had a lot of different chairman and directors and money men at Athletic over the years. When you saw a new case step out of his Jag, in a sheepskin coat with a cigar in his mouth, you knew we were going to go down. One chairman even went to jail. But then a new lot would take over and we'd go back up again.

* * *

A month after my illness was diagnosed, and while I was still thinking about how to kill Billy, Bangkok Rose's Mum came to visit from Thailand.

One evening when we were watching TV she said –I on the run from Cambodian hit man Arthur.–

–Don't look at me,– I replied. –I'm not running a safe house for people on the run. I sell photocopiers. If you want asylum go and see the police.–

–Never mind Arthur,– Rose said. –He's always on edge these days.–

Rose's Mum runs the *Bloods Head* bar in Bangkok and likes to visit her daughter in England from time to time. In some ways she has enough streetwise in her to pave a motorway, but in other ways she's a chuffing idiot. But we get on well and I'm always pleased to see her.

One morning I came downstairs for breakfast, after a night spent thinking of ways to whack Billy, to find the two of them at the kitchen table counting a pile of money they'd won at a casino in Leicester Square.

–How much you got there?–

–Never you mind,– said Rose. –Get your passport. We're going on a holiday. The taxi will be here in a minute.–

They sat in the back yakking away while I sat in the front with the driver. It was no use trying to tell them the obvious, they would find out soon enough.

At Heathrow we paid off the gold-toothed cabbie with the usual king's ransom, but inside the girls were surprised to find that going to Las Vegas post 9/11 wasn't like boarding a bus.

–You can't just buy a ticket like that Madam. You need a visa. You have to apply.–

–That's OK,– said Rose's Mum. –We not pay Visa, we pay cash.–

Voices rising.

–Madam, you need a visa.–

I could see an eye going out towards security and pulled the two disappointed gamblers away from the ticket counter. Unfortunately for them it was not going to be Las Vegas today.

We sat down and had a coffee. We were all suddenly deflated. I felt as badly as they did, a real party pooper. They had really been looking forward to going to Las Vegas.

So in a minute I jumped up and went over to the ticket counter. I asked the woman to find us the next plane that would take us to a city with a casino, that didn't need a visa.

She looked at me and then across at Bangkok Rose and her mum sitting there in their finery ready to go to Las Vegas.

In the end we got it all worked out. Bangkok Rose gave me a handful of notes and I booked three tickets on the next *QuikSnooze* flight to Amsterdam.

This immediately cheered them up. Bangkok Rose's Mum said she thought that her first husband had come from there and became very excited, but as we took a cab into the city and she didn't recognise anything she turned to me. –Guess I got it wrong Arthur. Think we live in Switzerland.–

After sighing and oohing and aahing at the canals and the trams and people on bicycles we dropped off at a casino, and after a quick gulp of bracing North Sea air Dutch style I escorted them inside.

Once they had got the hang of the currency and the tables they had no further use for me and I left them to it, two happy ladies, and went out to explore Amsterdam, eventually ending up at the Van Gogh museum.

That's what I like. A fellow obsessive. If someone had threatened his local football club he would have whacked the villain too. No doubt about it. There was a note in a guide that he'd never sold a picture in his lifetime. But that never stopped him.

I read the story about the Frenchwoman who was a hundred and something and still alive, who remembered him coming in to her store in the morning and how he had been a bad tempered bastard.

I knew how he felt. I'd have been pissed off if I'd produced a magic show like that and no one took any notice.

Two hours before the flight left I retrieved the girls and we took a cab back to the airport. They were still yakking. I glanced in the mirror and could see them counting their winnings.

Then I glanced at the driver, who had spotted them as well. He was a great square headed ex-Nazi type and I was just about to turn to the girls and say –Look out, we're not at home now, you're going to get clobbered,– when we drew up at the airport.

On the flight home they both fell fast asleep and I was left to watch the Dutch coast fall away below us and then a few minutes later the English coast appear. As we came in to land I felt a sharp twist in my guts, which was a marker telling me that my time was limited.

* * *

I told Frank about my plan to kill Billy while we were having a drink at the *Albert Arms*.

Frank had been our centre forward when we'd won the Terrier's Dog Food Cup at Wembley, the greatest day in the club's history. He was also my best friend. I could see he needed to be convinced.

–So what would you say if I shot Hitler?– I asked.

–Hero,– he replied.

–Stalin?–

–Top dog. Knighthood.–

–Jack the Ripper.–

–Ditto.–

–Billy Petersen?–

Frank looked at me.

–Yeah,– he said after a while. –I get the point you're making. But what about children, family?–

–You worried about Hitler's kids?–

–No. But Billy's offspring could have been geniuses. Concert pianists or scientists. You've snuffed out a whole line.–

–You're wrong Frank,– I said. –Follow the DNA.–

I numbered the odds off on my fingers. –It's 1000/1 Mother Teresa, 100/1 the concert pianist, 2/1 the greedy nutjob.–

–Gotcha. You're doing a public service.–

–We should make a list, set up a web site. 'Whack a Tyrant for Jesus,' that sort of thing. They should give me an MBE. I'm only doing my duty.–

–What about an African dictator?–

–What about him?–

–You're always banging on about poverty. What about whacking the bloke in the leopard skin hat who stole all the oil money?–

–Peanuts, small fry.–

–What?–

–No point. Small ripple. Small pond. Everyone expects a case like that to get whacked.–

–But not Billy Petersen.–

–Nooohhh. Big ripple. Big pond. Imagine the head-lines. BILLY WHACKED! That would run for ever.–

–You'd be Lee Harvey Oswald.–

–Now you've got it!–

–Jesus, Arthur, you want to watch yourself.–

* * *

We had other obsessions as well.

We, that's me and Rose, Frank and Nancy, Smithy the Traveller, Nell, Benny the Jeweller and Stan the Owl and a few others, dreamt of inventing a game that would make us millionaires.

Smithy came home from a trip to Italy and said he'd seen a game on TV where housewives stripped off their tops if they got a question wrong. He kept on going on about it until I could see Nell beginning to brew up so I had to tell him to can it.

Then Frank came into the *Albert Arms* one evening with this small box he'd picked up in the market in Morocco. He'd gone there on a motorbike rally with Nancy.

The box looked like it was hand made and inside there were two dice.

We couldn't work out what it was made from so we took it down to Benny the Jeweller who tapped and scraped and then said he thought it was probably camel bone.

The dice had been cut from quartz and the dots were painted on in faded yellow which we thought represented the desert sand or the sun.

The dice were irregular in shape but when Benny weighed and tested them he said they were as perfectly balanced as any dice produced in a factory here.

He rolled them round and round in his hand.

–I can't explain it,– he said, looking over the top of his glasses. –Whoever cut these isn't just a crafts-man, he's a magician.–

* * *

We called the game Sure Start Holidays and got Nell to type up the rules. Instead of planning a holiday you went to the airport and let the dice decide for you. Dozey Dave, who worked behind the bar at the *Albert Arms*, volunteered to be our guinea pig.

We took him out to Heathrow and over lunch in Harry Ramsden's he threw a six and a four which put him on the next plane to Belgium. Then we went home. We thought he'd do a short tour of Europe and then fly home and have his two weeks in Blackpool.

A week later we had a telephone call to say he'd followed the rules and arrived in Murmansk and was enjoying himself.

A month after that we got a card saying he was going out with a local girl and there has been no more since then. Albert has replaced him with an illegal immigrant from Syria called Hassan and life has continued.

–Looks like the game works,– Frank said.

–But they're supposed to come back,– I replied.

–That's right,– Frank said in a puzzled tone. –So they are.–

* * *

We appointed Smithy the Traveller our Expert Adviser on Sure Start Holidays.

There are a lot of people who can't work Smithy out. When we were at school someone said that his mum and dad were high up Communist spies and that every time they got a letter they had to eat it after they read it in case it contained a secret message.

Smithy's Mum lives in Cornwall now. Smithy said mysteriously the other day –She's writing her memoirs. It's all going to come out then.–

But he won't say anything more. Smithy loves a mystery.

Smithy says he's a revolutionary too but when he

comes into the *Albert Arms* with the ratty dog he always has with him he looks more like he sells the Big Issue.

But we appointed him our Expert Adviser because every so often he disappears for months before turning up again at the *Albert Arms* with tales of mining for silver in South America or being a reporter in Bosnia or Iraq.

–Where you been this time Smithy?– someone will call out.

–Vietnam or Morocco or the Amazon jungle.–

–What was the weather like Smithy.–

–Hot, cold, wet, indifferent.–

–Any cannibals Smithy?–

–Only right here!–

He calls himself the *Albert Arms* Travel Consultant now. But if we used half his suggestions none of the people would ever come back.

–Tell 'em to fry a scorpion in the desert.

–Make 'em walk a thousand miles due North.

–Get 'em to boil an egg in the Andes.–

* * *

With an education Frank would have got somewhere. He was as sharp as a tin tack on the internet. He soon had all the info we needed on Billy.

–Every night he goes into the *Tombola* office at 10.00 pm and stays until midnight. Then he goes to the private room at the back of an exclusive casino. Leaves between 2.00 am and 2.30 am.–

–Timing always the same?–

–Never varies. He comes down the back stairway. A driver pulls up outside the side entrance and he gets into the car. That's the time to make the hit.–

–Thanks Frank.–

* * *

Frank had been a natural striker of the ball. He was quick, with two good feet and he could head the ball as well. Arsenal looked at him several times. But Frank was a home boy. That was why we liked him. Everyone knew that he was Athletic through and through.

He made his debut away at Bristol City. Christ knows where he got the idea from, but when they came trotting out onto the pitch there were ten of them with ordinary coloured hair and one with bright lemon coloured hair.

I looked up to where two of our directors were sitting and I thought you're an arse Frank, you're stuffed before you start.

But he scored two goals and after the game the chairman put his arm around him for the photographers and the Ratcatchers put a picture in the paper with the headline:

THE LEMON HEAD KID HITS TOWN!

Frank had ten good seasons with Athletic. He never let the club down once. But he never got the wages he should have. I remember the game when he got injured.

We were at Notts County and their centre half was a brute of a bloke who clattered into him and he went down hard. He went off between the trainer and the physio and I turned to Nell and said –That looks serious. –

He was out for a month and he was never the same when he came back. He'd lost a yard in pace and was slow on the turn.

We had a crooked lot running the club at the time

and he didn't get a proper pay off. He got a settlement in the end, but he had to threaten to take them to court.

After he finished playing and because of his injury he began to put on weight. Some people started to call him Fat Frank but I never did. I had too much respect for him.

He invested the pay off he got from Athletic in a motorcycle dealership. Now he and Nancy are always off on a motor bike somewhere dressed up in their black leathers. It was while they were in Morocco on a rally that they found the box.

* * *

We'd all grown up together, Frank, me, Smithy, Nell and the others. Athletic was our education. Who except for our lot could tell you anything about Huddersfield or Lincoln or Bristol?

We went everywhere with the team. We even went to Devon when they had a pre-season tour there playing local sides. We sat on Plymouth Hoe and ate pasties and made daft jokes about Francis Drake playing bowls.

Nell organised all the travel. Most of the time she could get us there and back in a day.

–If the bookies ever packs up Nell,– I said, –they'd give you a job in a travel agents any day.–

We went all over. I remember the day we went to Hull.

Smithy the Traveller had just got a new dog and he wanted to bring it with us. Nell sorted it out with the train but when we got to the ground there was a woman on the gate and she wouldn't let it in. It was pissing with rain and Smithy said –One more dog in this place won't make any difference,– and the old baggage looked at him and said that if he didn't clear off she'd call the police.

So we all went in while Smithy went to the pub with his dog and started to chat with a group of Danish fisherman who'd put in to do some repairs to their boat.

When we came out of the game we ganged up with them and went to a Chinese. There was a bit of a wrangle at the door over the dog, but there were a dozen of us by this time and I could see they needed the trade so in the end they let us in.

The dog went under the table and every so often when another dish came out someone would lift the table cloth and peer under and then say something like –Just checking to make sure the dog's still got all his legs,– and we'd all give a laugh.

After we'd finished the Danes invited us back to their boat and we spent the rest of the evening yakking about this and that. In the end it turned out that Smithy knew more Denmark than the Danes did!

After that we forgot all about getting the train home and just put our heads down anywhere we could find a space.

In the morning when we'd woken up and cleared our heads we realised that Nell was missing. It was Smithy who found her doubled up in a bunk in a cabin with the Danish skipper.

On the way home in the train she said –You tell anyone, Arthur Polianski, and I'll rip the balls off you.–

And none of us did. We were good like that.

Though every so often Smithy or someone would say something like –I wonder what the weather's like in Denmark this morning,– and get a dirty look from Nell.

When we were at school we used to call her Smelly Nelly after she tipped a bottle of her mother's perfume over herself and stank the class out. But you wouldn't dare call her that now. She works in the bookies run by her uncle Stan the Owl.

A lot of people said we should have got together. I've always fancied her, especially when she gives me a hug and presses her big bazookas into me. But you can't get off with your best mate can you?

* * *

And anyway before I linked up with Rose I'd never been short of women. I'd always had all sorts of opportunities.

I was in and out and all over the place. I'd fix a photocopier in the council or in the library or install a new one in an office somewhere.

Sometimes you'd get a Mrs Hacksaw who wanted to know the ins and outs of everything and would never even offer you a glass of water.

But most times you got a secretary bird who was glad of a chat. You'd sort out whatever was wrong and then Polly or Daisy or whoever would say –Fancy a coffee Arthur?–

And you'd say why not and you'd have a yak and if she was half decent you might ask her out.

One day I had a call out to an office. I had a funny feeling about it as soon as I stepped into the lift.

She wasn't the normal secretary. She had an air about her. She had half moon specs and her hair done up at the back and her office was the size of most people's front rooms.

I didn't say anything and set to work, but I could see her looking over at me and I thought hello.

So when'd I'd finished and she said, in a cut glass

accent –Would you like a coffee Mr Polianksi? I'm just making one.–

I replied –Well why not then.–

She opened the door to the office.

–Do come in, Eric's out, he won't mind.–

A minute later I was perched on the edge of a sofa in an office the size of a football pitch, coffee cup in hand and she was fiddling round in a room at the back.

I'd just glanced down and was wondering where you asked a money like this out to when I looked up and saw her standing in front of me stark naked, with no clothes on, and a idiot grin on her face.

–So how do you take your women, Mr Polinaski?– she said, giving me a twirl. –From the front or the back?–

At which point I dropped the coffee cup and it shattered into a thousand ming pieces. As it hit the wooden floor she started to shriek and I was running out of the office, thinking that Eric was in the back room with a shotgun, not taking the elevator but the stairs four at a time. A minute later I was standing in the street outside, looking up at the office window where she was standing, still stark naked, waving her fist and shouting at me.

I told Frank about it in the pub that night.

–You should have gone for it Arthur,– he said. –Rutting the secretary on the chairman's desk! You get your photo on the wall for that.–

I told him not to be an arse and said she was a nutjob and not to tell anyone.

But of course the following night Smithy the Traveller said –I hear you've been poking the bourgeoisie Arthur,– which set everybody off.

* * *

Rose said I was becoming worse.

–Since you had the news from the doctor you've been all over the place.–

I looked at her. –When the doctor tells you you're dying it concentrates the mind, Rose. You haven't got time for messing about. You get on with things.–

And I had done everything I was supposed to do. I had sorted out the house and insurances. She would be alright with money.

I hadn't told her about my plan to whack Billy. She thought it was just the football or the music or dancing.

I'd hear a song on the radio and I'd spend all day hunting it down. Then I'd listen to it over and over.

I could dance too. Rose said I was the best dancer at the *Trocadero* by a million miles.

When she took me to see the Billy Elliot film about the dancer she said –That should've been you Arthur.–

And she was right. Out on the dance floor, the rhythm of the music went through me like a current of electricity.

Benny went to Israel on holiday and came back with a CD of Jewish folk songs that I played for days on end until Rose said –That music's driving me mad Arthur. Bin it or I walk.–

So now I only play it when she's out.

I understood the serious music too. I could go into the church in Leipzig and say to Johann Sebastian Bach –How do you manage when you wake up every morning hearing God talking to the Angels inside your head? How do you find time to talk to your wife or get a haircut or make a cup of tea?–

But best of all I liked the CD Smithy the Traveller brought back from Africa of a group of Congolese drummers. Listening to them was like being plugged into the mains. They turned my skin inside out. Those beefs knew everything there was to know about music. In fact I got so excited about it I even took the CD down to Athletic.

–That's the sort of music the team should be running out to,– I told Ron the commercial director. –That would inspire anyone.–

I persuaded him to put it on the tannoy and we listened to it full blast from the centre circle.

He smiled and shook his head.

–Now, now, young Arthur,– he said finally as we walked back to the stand, –we don't want anyone ending up in the cooking pot do we?–

As I said to Rose that night –They're so wet down there they'll come out dressed as fairies next.–

* * *

I went on a recce. I was serious now, I told you. Any time I faltered I just felt my stomach and imagined what was growing there.

For three nights I sat in the corner window of the McDonald's across the street and watched Billy's Jag draw up. It arrived on the dot of two. The driver cut the lights and waited. Every so often he looked in the rear view mirror but I never saw him turn around or look over his shoulder.

Billy came down between two and two thirty. He had a bodyguard who was always on his right hand side, opening the back door of the car for him. I noted that the bodyguard always looked forward toward the open square rather than back up the street.

* * *

One evening I was in the *Albert Arms* and I decided to ask Stan the Owl a hypothetical.

–Stan,– I said. –Suppose you were dying of cancer and you had the chance to rid the world of a greedy nutjob. What would you do?–

Mumble, mumble, fag ash, fag ash.

Stan the Owl, who wore round spectacles and had a round face, was Nell's uncle and he ran the betting shop. When he went to the races he wore a trilby hat and a three piece suit.

He always had fag ash on his waistcoat and he mumbled so you had to listen if you wanted to understand him. There were a lot of people who thought they could put one over on Stan because of the way he looked. But at the end of the day it was Stan who usually came out on top.

At one time he'd been a lawyer, but there had been a problem with a case so he'd packed it in and taken up with the betting shop instead. But you could always go to him if you wanted to know something legal.

One time Smithy went to South America to prospect in a silver mine there. But he hadn't realised that if he wanted to go prospecting for silver in South America he needed a licence, which he didn't have, so they threw him in jail.

So he telephoned Nell, who spoke to Stan, who it turned out had spent time in South America when he was a young man and could speak Spanish and knew about South American law. So he went out there leaving Nell to run the betting shop and had Smithy out of jail in twenty four hours.

After that they went on a bit of a carouse visiting Stan's old haunts. When they came home a couple of months later, Stan had lost two stone in weight and caught a dose of the clap.

Nell wanted to throw him out of the house she was so angry, until he reminded her whose house it was.

Smithy was so thin that when he came into the *Albert Arms* with his dog it was difficult to know which was him and which was the dog, they were both so undernourished and ratty.

I bought him a drink and repeated the question.

–You're on your way out and you've got the chance to get rid of a greedy nutjob. What do you do?–

He leaned toward me and mumbled something that sounded like –Shoot the fucker!–

And then he got up and walked out.

* * *

One day a man from the brewery came to the *Albert Arms* and said to Albert that the brewery was brewing a new beer and that they were holding a competition to give it a name. He said it was a strong brew with a nutty taste.

So I said –Why not call it Tiger's Knob?– which got a laugh.

But Stan the Owl, when he thought Albert wasn't listening, said if it was strong and nutty they should call it Albert's Wife, which got a laugh as well.

But then Smithy had a slurp, banged his glass down on the bar and said out loud –Parsons Pond.– Just like that, and we all roared with laughter.

Mr Parsons had been the English teacher at school who stood up in assembly one morning and said if he had his time again he would have read Shakespeare in the lunch hour rather than play football.

Miss Pond was the gym mistress who always wore a track suit and could do as many press ups as Frank.

Then one day in assembly they were both missing and the head announced they'd been sacked after they'd been found on top of each other in the staff room.

After that someone said Miss Pond had gone to work in a brothel and that Mr Parsons was in prison.

But then a month later Nell was in the High Street shopping when she bumped into Miss Pond who said she had got a job as manageress in Dorothy Perkins and was much happier, and that Mr Parsons was working in an off licence.

In the end the brewery brought in a team of management consultants who called the new beer Super Strength Number One, but as far as we were all concerned it was always –A pint of Parsons Pond please Albert!–

* * *

After three nights watching from the McDonald's I moved across the street.

Three paces back from the club exit I found a sheltered doorway. That night, wearing dark clothes, I walked up the street just before two and hid in the doorway. At bang on two Billy's Jag drew up. I was hidden in the doorway out of sight. Even if the driver looked over his shoulder he wouldn't see me. There was a light over the club exit, but the nearest street lamp was fifty yards down the road toward the square.

Inching forward I saw the rear end of the Jag. The driver had the window down and I could hear the radio and smell his cigarette. A minute later he got out and opened the back door of the car.

Then the exit door of the club opened and Billy's sleek silver head, scarf, and thick overcoat passed almost in front of me as he dipped down into the back seat. He was perfectly lit.

The bodyguard, who had accompanied him down the stairs, got in to the passenger seat on the other side, the door slammed and they drove off.

The following day I discreetly paced out the distance from the doorway where I had hidden to the car. Three good paces, no more.

* * *

One evening in the *Albert Arms* Frank said –Supposing, hypothetically speaking, I had a son. Would you recommend that he go into the photocopying business then Arthur?–
I could see immediately that he was taking the piss.
So I replied –I'll bring one down here and wrap it round your neck if you carry on like that Frank!–
Laughter all round.
But there are a lot of things you've got to learn if you want to make a living selling photocopiers.
I tried to explain it to Smithy one evening when he was having a drink with Nell. Frank was off on his bike somewhere with Nancy.
–You're not just selling a machine,– I said. –You're selling an experience.–
–What, like going to Alton Towers or summat?– said Nell, playing dumb.
–That's right,– I replied. –You don't want it to be too simple. People want to feel they've got their money's worth. Say the boss comes down with a bunch of boring black and white nonsense. Well that's when secretary bird jumps into action. Burrrrdummm. Alter the format, a touch of bold, a bit of zoom, a *soupçon* of colour and *voilà,* out the other end comes a document so dazzling you have to put sunglasses on to read it!–
–Gotcha,– said Smithy.
I looked round to make sure we weren't being spied on and then leaned forward and said to the pair of them darkly –We've added a few other extras as well!–

–What's that?– they said in chorus.

I leaned forward again.

–Don't tell anyone, but the latest thing is a mini step-ladder so the secretaries can get up and photocopy their bums at Christmas!–

–Get away,– they chorused again. –You're joking!–

–I'm not,– I said. –They even send copies to New York by email!–

The pair of them sat back in stunned silence. Then I walked over to the bar and said to Albert the Landlord in a loud voice –There's some silly chuffers round here who'll believe anything.–

* * *

But it wasn't often I had a laugh. Most of the time I was angry.

If a Martian landed, he wouldn't see what I see.

He wouldn't see people eating Chinese takeaways, or going to the football, or buying villas in Spain. No, he'd see a bloody miserable place. I did my research into the real state of the world.

I rang Frank.

–Guess what?–

–What?–

–There's fifteen thousand children a day dying from starvation while the rest of us are as fat as pigs.–

Silence. Sound of eating. I tried again.

–There's thousands of children dying every year from diarrhoea because they can't afford a treatment that costs only a few pence.–

Silence. Sound of eating again.

Then Frank said –Sounds like a load of shite to me.–

I slammed down the phone.

I went to the reference library and read everything I could find about Billy Petersen and his companies.

When I discovered that because of an accountancy fiddle *Tombola* had paid no tax at all last year I shouted –FUCK OFF!– as loud as I could, causing the swivel eyed bitch at the counter to turn and give me a death-ray look. But I didn't care. I ran out of the library to the phone booth across the road and telephoned Frank.

–Guess what.–

–We're eating our dinner.–

–We?–

–Rose is here.–

–Rose? What's she doing there?–

–Wondering where you are Arthur.–

–Right. I've been in the library.–

–Doing what?–

–Research.–

–What you found out?–

I took a deep breath.

–In the last year *Tombola* didn't pay any tax at all. Not a penny. Zero. Zilch. Not even a round lady's bum.–

There was a pause, then Frank shouted –SHOOT THE FUCKER!– and slammed down the phone.

* * *

–What are you doing on the computer all day? Looking at porn?–

–No, I'm buying a gun.–

Clack, clack, clack.

Rose appeared at the top of the stairs.

–What do you want a gun for Arthur? I thought you and Frank were inventing a game?–

–We are. I'm multi tasking. I'm doing two things at once.–

A minute later I could hear her on the phone to her mother.

* * *

The trouble with buying a gun, I told Frank as I looked at the bottom of my pint glass, is that it's too damn easy.

–How long?–

–Thirteen minutes.–

–With ammo?–

–The lot.–

–Not bad!–

We'd played games like this before.

I'd bet Frank a fish and chip supper he couldn't book a holiday in Murmansk in under ten minutes. He'd done it in seven.

–Too easy,– he said, as he scoffed the chips.

–Rose's Mum says she can have Billy whacked for a grand.–

–Rose's Mum is mad. You'll have Mr Plod in your lap before you start. You've got to do it yourself.–

–Right.–

I went to an internet café and ordered the gun, paying for it with a credit card of my mum's that I'd kept going after she died just in case I needed it.

Then I paid Hassan, Dozey Dave's replacement behind the bar at the *Albert Arms*, £100 to open a PO Box for me and collect the gun when it arrived.

–What happens if they open the parcel?–

–Tell them it's for my mum.–

* * *

Rose worked as a care assistant at the *Suk U Dry* Care and Rest Home. The home was run by a tall thin beef called Hemlock who had a beard, rode everywhere on a bicycle and was known as the most miserable man who ever walked the face of the earth.

One evening we were in the *Albert Arms*. There was just me and Rose and Frank and Nancy and Stan the Owl and Nell and Smithy. Rose suddenly started to giggle.

–What's up Rose,– I said. –Got a pork scratching stuck up your nose?– I was angry with her because she was starting to put on weight again.

–I can't help it Arthur,– she replied, –I was just thinking about what's happening at work.–

–What's that then Rose?– asked Frank.

–It's Hemlock. He's feeding the residents dog biscuits. They're special energy ones for greyhounds. He's got half a ton of them out the back.–

We turned and gawped at her.

Then Smithy shouted –Jesus. I knew it. Call the police. Burn the nutjob out.–

–No, you've got it wrong Smithy. The residents love them. He gives them out as cereal at breakfast with milk and sugar.–

–And ...–

We all leaned forward.

–Well,– said Rose. She was trying to control herself but she was beginning to shake like a jelly. –After breakfast they go back to their rooms and you can hear the walls shaking. We think there's Viagra in the biscuits. By lunchtime they're exhausted and they spend the afternoons slumped in their chairs in front of the telly. Then in the evening its bingo and yak, yak, yak ... Winston Churchill and who won the war and beer at tuppence a pint. They're having the time of their lives. He's got a list of people waiting to get in.–

–Jesus.–

I woke up in the middle of the night, feeling the pain in my stomach and thinking about dog biscuits and Viagra and the *Suk U Dry* Care and Rest Home.

The next day I said to Rose –If Hemlock's such a clever bastard, why isn't he riding round in a Rolls Royce like every other care home owner?–

–Search me Arthur. He's such a nutjob he probably buries it all in the back garden.–

* * *

Rose had been badgering me, so one Saturday afternoon I took her to the football. I knew it was a mistake as soon as we walked into the ground.

The chairman had sold our star striker to buy a new villa in Spain and we had slipped out of the League and into the Conference. It was raining cats and dogs. The crowd was rubbish, no more than five hundred, and the game was rubbish too.

I looked at the rusty old stand and felt angry that they had let the club slide. For the first time, I saw the ground for what it had become.

There was a time when I was so proud of this place I thought my heart would jump out of my chest. But I looked around at it now, all rusty and rickety in the rain with a team who couldn't score a goal if you paid them.

At half time I bought Rose a pie and she took one look at it and threw it in the bin.

–What are you trying to do Arthur, poison me?–

I couldn't blame her. I looked at the sodden mess in the bin with the rain trickling down on to it. After that we left.

On the way out we passed Jack the Gateman. –I can't take any more Jack,– I said. –It breaks my heart.–

–I know what you mean Arthur,– he replied. –I'd leave as well if I could.–

He half turned, as if pulling some imaginary string that held him.

I remembered the times we'd marked out the pitch together. We'd discuss the next game. We were proud of our team then.

We shook hands.

–Be seeing you Jack.–

–Yeah, be seeing you Arthur.–

I went back the odd time but it was never the same. I guess it was my illness that was colouring everything, but somehow it was as if the scales had fallen from my eyes.

But don't get me wrong. If anybody had ever asked me –Arthur Polianski, what's the most important thing in your life?–

I'd have replied –Athletic,– without any hesitation at all.

* * *

A week after I took Rose to Athletic I found myself in church. It must have been a Sunday but I don't know how I got there. I stood up and sat down with the others. I was captivated by the singing, the candles, the voices. Even the smell and the shape of the place touched me. I stared at the light as it poured in through the stained glass windows.

I'm not a nutjob. I don't believe Jesus Christ rose from his grave after three days any more than I believe in Father Christmas. But at the same time, there was something about the church that touched me deeply.

Suddenly an old woman tapped me on the shoulder and whispered –You alright love?–

And I realised there were tears streaming down my face.

* * *

And so the days passed. I got used to the idea of dying. I knew when it was going to happen. I could prepare myself.

Rose said she was prepared too. We talked of going on a cruise or a trip to Thailand to see her mum.

Sometimes we'd talk about the doctor with the piggy eyes who had given me the death sentence.

–How many times a week do you reckon he does that Rose?–

–I dunno. Three, four?–

–They should at least have someone to give you a cup of tea. Not put you straight back out on the street. It's not fair the way it is!–

I started to go to church regularly. I didn't try to work out why. I was fed up with thinking about things. I just found it a calming influence.

I said to Rose –Why don't you come with me?–

–I'm a chuffing Buddhist, remember?–

–Yeah, right.–

* * *

One evening we were all in the *Albert Arms* when Smithy told us he had been in the siege of Sarajevo. He said they'd cooked up dogs and cats to eat.

I glanced down at the ratty animal by his feet.

Then Frank said –Why do you do it Smithy? Why do you end up in crazy places like Sarajevo?–

–Because I'd rather spend a day there than a life-time in a place like this,– Smithy replied, looking round the bar. After that he told us that *Tombola* had signed him up as a war correspondent in Sarajevo and told him to interview a beauty queen who'd been raped.

Pause. Then Nell asked –What should we do with Billy, Smithy?–

–Shoot the fucker!–

Frank and I exchanged glances.

Smithy's a walking encyclopaedia.

–Where you going next Smithy?–

–Arabia, Mt Everest.–

–Can we come with you Smithy?–

–FUCK OFF!–

Smithy always bangs on about places no one's ever heard of.

–Do you know there's a tribe in the Amazon jungle that doesn't have a word for tomorrow?–

–Sounds like round here!–

Or

–I saw a man in Murmansk frozen to death after he took out his willy for a slash in the middle of winter.–

–You should get together with Mexican Pete. He's the new DJ down at the *Trocadero.* He used to be a bullfighter in Spain. You'd get on well.–

–Oh yeah.–

* * *

After a while we all became Billy experts. We were all involved. There was Rose and me, Frank and Nancy, Nell, Smithy the Traveller, Stan the Owl and Benny the Jeweller.

When we'd done our researches we had a meeting at the *Albert Arms*. I hadn't told them that I planned to kill Billy. As far as they were concerned we were just gathering information.

–There's no doubt that *Tombola* is the jewel of Billy's empire,– Nell began. –It gave him the cash to buy his magazines in Africa.–

–How many magazines has he got then?– I asked.

–More than a hundred,– Nell replied.

I tried to think what an African magazine would look

like and if it would be printed in black and white or colour.

–But its not just papers and magazines he owns in Africa,– Stan said. –We've found out that he owns diamond mines as well.–

After that it was Frank's turn.

–Lifestyle in London?– I asked.

–Lavish,– he replied.

–Generous?–

–Tight as a duck's arse.–

–Servants?–

–Female. African.–

–Accommodation?–

–Four storey. Two toilets per floor. King size double bed in each bedroom. Black sheets. Private cinema. Gym. Special Ratcatchers entrance at the back. Vomitorium.–

–Vomitorium?–

–It's a special room the Romans invented. An African servant sticks her fingers down your throat to make you sick so you can go back and gorge yourself again with the rest of them.–

–Jesus.–

I turned to Smithy. –Mental condition?–

–Compulsive, ultra aggressive, borderline paranoiac and kleptomaniac.–

–Comparisons?–

–Hitler, Stalin.–

–Give over Smithy,– said Frank. –They killed millions.–

–So would he if you gave him a tank. He's raped and pillaged in Africa along with the rest of them.–

–Examples please, Smithy.–

–Last year. *The Daily African.* They write a story saying Africa's starving and the rich countries have pinched everything and he shuts it down on the spot. No pay off, no redundancy, no nothing. Fit ones go to the council dump picking garbage. Women and children join the sex industry.–

–And the diamond mines?–

–He's got a goon squad that goes from mine to mine. Any trouble or they get behind with production and they cut your arm off.–

–Jesus. Wife?–

–Ex. Swedish glamour puss.–

–Dripping in diamonds?–

–Correct.–

–Mistresses?–

–Two. One African, one Chinese.–

–Dripping in diamonds?–

–Correct.–

–So why did he leave Norway?–

–He'd bought everything they had to sell.–

–Influence?–

–Open door to Prime Ministers and Presidents.–

–Future plans?–

–*Tombola TV* begins next year.–

–Long term prognosis?–

–Will continue to expand unless stopped.–

–Health?–

–Medics pummel and poke regularly. Say he is a very fit beef for his age.–

–Sum it up Smithy.–

–He's the wild dog who escaped the pack.–

* * *

We drew up our bill of indictment against Billy. It was a belter.

Article 1. Underpayment Of Tax. Nell and Stan worked it out down at the bookies. On *Tombola's* turnover Billy should have been forking out millions. Actual amount paid? Zero, zilch, not a bean. Not even a round lady's bum.

–It gets better than that,– I said.

–What does?–

–Listen and you'll find out.–

–He's even getting a FUCKING REBATE!–

–He's even getting a FUCKING WHAT?–

–They're giving him a tax break to help him knock down the ground!–

–Give me a gun, I'll shoot the fucker myself.–

Smithy says that's what they do in China. The family of an executed criminal has to pay for his bullet.

Article 2. Rank Hypocrisy. Telling everybody else they've got to behave when acting like a total shite-hawk himself.

Article 3. Poisoning The Well Of Society. This is according to Smithy. He says there are well documented cases of people killing themselves after Billy's Ratcatchers threatened to expose them. Smithy says they should change the name from *Tombola* to the *Daily Blackmail.*

Article 4. Threatened Closure And Total Wrecking of Athletic Football Club (AFC).

* * *

I came into the *Albert Arms* one evening and Hassan signalled me over to the bar.

–I've got your parcel Arthur.–

I waited for him to hand it over.

–You've got to pay me Arthur.–

I handed him a couple of notes and he reached under the bar and came up with my parcel.

I checked the postmark, America. Thankfully it was a plain wrapper.

As I said to Frank later –It's surprising how easy these things are.–

–Yeah,– he said, –there should be a law against it.–

We both laughed.

I waited until Rose was out before I opened the parcel in the bedroom.

Without thinking I had been expecting a Roy Rogers style sharpshooter, all silver and pearl, but this was different. It was the business. It was small and dark, fitting nicely in the hand with a comfortable heaviness. I fitted the silencer and wondered what to do next.

–Frank, I've ...–

–Don't talk on the phone Arthur.–

–Why not?–

–Security.–

–Oh.–

I hid the gun under the bed along with the box of ammunition.

Next evening Frank came to pick me up in the van.

–Day of the Jackal,– I said as I climbed in, holding the shopping bag that contained the gun.

–They were fresh out of melons at the Co-op.–

We both laughed.

Sitting in the van in a lay-by we plotted the way ahead.

* * *

The greatest day in Athletic's history was when we won the Terrier's Dog Food Cup at Wembley. Us at Wembley! I had to pinch myself to make sure it wasn't a dream.

I knew as I began to surface that it was a special

day. It could have been Christmas Day or even my birthday. But then as the fog of sleep cleared I came awake suddenly. It was The Day Of The Match. I got out of bed, rubbed my face and looked at myself in the mirror.

–It's a big day Arthur boy,– I said. –You've got to be prepared.–

I met the others and we had a fry up in a café before we left. On the train we were talking ten to the dozen, but as we walked up Wembley Way we suddenly went quiet. It was like being in church.

–Chuffing hell,– I said in a whisper to Nell. –I can't believe we're here.–

They reckon that most finals are a disappointment, but this one was a belter. All the TV people were there.

I nudged Nell. –That's Trevor Brooking down there.–
–Never mind that,– she said. –Look up.–

I did and saw John Motson looking back down at me! At half time it was 1-1 and we were hoarse from shouting.

Frank's Dad opened his thermos and turned to me. –It's all right Arthur,– he said, –we're going to win. I had a dream.–

Frank's Dad was like that. He was always having dreams. –It ends 2-1. Frank scores in the last minute.–
And he was right.

After the match we went back to the *Albert Arms* where they showed highlights of the game on TV and we cheered ourselves hoarse again.

–Day of my life Arthur,– said Frank's Dad. –Better than my wedding day.–

I looked over to where Franks's Mum was sitting.

–I should watch what you say there mate.– I nodded over to where she was sitting. –That one can lip read.–

Frank, or the Lemon Head Kid as everyone called him then, came in later with some of the other players. We roared ourselves hoarse when he stood on a chair in front of the bar and held up the cup.

After that we did a conga round the downstairs of the pub and we'd have gone upstairs too, only Albert's Wife barred the way. After that we all got to hold the cup.

I held it up with Nell. Me holding up a cup! Someone took a photo of us and later it was pinned up behind the bar.

Then Frank's Mum came over to me and said –Frank's Dad's gone missing.–

So we went outside to look for him and found him sitting on a wall muttering –My boy's won the cup, my boy's won the cup.–

That was the beginning of the end for him. Frank's Mum reckoned it was the excitement that set it off. In six months he was in a home barely able to talk. One day I went to visit and he thought I was Jesus Christ. A month later he was dead.

* * *

We held other meetings to decide what to do about Billy. Smithy said we needed some revolutionary slogans to inspire us. So we had several T-shirts made up.

We had one printed with the slogan BALLS TO BILLY! on the front.

Another had a Billy character, drawn cartoon style, pissing on an outline of the continent of Africa.

Then one day Smithy came into the *Albert Arms* carrying a large shoulder bag.

He opened it up and pulled out two giant flags which he said his mum had made up for him in Cornwall.

The inscription on the first flag read:

*Those with Benefit Books shall be given Rolls
Royces,
And those with Rolls Royces shall be given Benefit
Books.*

The inscription on the second flag read:

*And the Journalists shall become Ratcatchers,
And the Ratcatchers shall become Journalists.*

–We should drape them over the side of the stadium,–
Smithy said, looking around, daring anyone to challenge him. –That'll show the nutjobs that we mean
business.–

* * *

In the end it was General Blair who gave me my
justification for whacking Billy.

It was one evening when we were watching TV and
he came on to tell us why we had to attack the
Arabs.

He said if someone threatens to whack you, you've
got to get in and whack them first.

I nodded and said to Rose –That case has got it
right. If it was me I'd hang 'em all up by their knob
ends.–

We sat and listened.

Then I said –Do you ever wonder what he's like first
thing in the morning, when he's brushing his teeth
and looking at himself in the mirror?–

Rose stared at the screen for a second and then said
–No, never.– And getting up she went into the
kitchen to make a cup of tea.

So she missed the next bit of his speech when he said he was going to start up a new war, but this time it was going to be a Campaign Against Pig Ignorance And People Who Can't Read.

That set everyone off.

For days you couldn't turn on the telly or open the paper without someone saying the English had got pork scratchings for brains and that the French could read and write by the time they were two and that the Italians could rut in ten different languages. Even the Welsh got in on the act, saying we'd ruined their language for them, until someone on the TV asked –So how do you say We Rut Sheep in Welsh?–

After which they had to shut up.

General Blair said everyone had to play their part in his Campaign Against Pig Ignorance And People Who Can't Read.

So one day the head beef at *Krap U Luv* said he was going to change the name of his stores from *Krap U Luv* to *You Love Crap.*

That got everyone yakking and then some beef in a university who'd swallowed a dictionary said –What you want to do is decline the name.–

When this was explained to the head beef he said he'd nail the case to a cross if he was taking the piss, but then the other beefs in the universities reckoned it was a good idea, so soon every *KUL* store in the country had a flickering grammar lesson stuck to its front end.

> I Love Crap,
> You Love Crap,
> He Loves Crap ...

And so on.

To begin with it was a novelty. People stood outside the stores and chanted the phrases as if they were at a football match.

Someone even said Cliff Richard should turn it into a song.

But then people got bored and began to boo and make monkey noises and throw bottles at the flickering lights.

Finally the doctors announced that the lights were giving children epileptic fits and *KUL* had to close half its stores in Scotland to pay the compensation to the families.

After that the head beef resigned and went to live in Spain with his secretary and the stores reverted to their old name.

I thought about what the General had said in his TV interview, that he was right to whack the Arabs because they were wild dogs. I reckoned that meant I was right to whack Billy Petersen, because he was a wild dog too.

* * *

Bangkok Rose's Mum has connections, and ex-husbands, everywhere. One day when she was visiting I came home from work to find a gang of Thai men redecorating the house.

–Mum's been watching one of the makeover programmes on TV,– Rose said.

When I went outside I saw they were on the roof too.

–What are they doing on the roof, Rose?–

–They're putting up a new satellite dish. Mum wants to watch Thai TV.–

But it wasn't just the Thai TV we got. We ended up with French, German, Italian. One day I came home to find them watching the news from New Zealand.

A week later I was upstairs on the internet checking a site that explained the correct way to hold a gun when the doorbell rang.

I heard Rose answer it. She came to the foot of the stairs and shouted up –There's a policeman here. He wants to see you.–

–Christ.–

I looked at the site and then over to the gun and the ammunition lying on the bed.

I pulled the plug on the computer and went to the top of the stairs.

–Tell him I'm having a bath.–

Clack, clack, clack.

–He says you've to come down straight away.–

–Christ.–

I went into the bedroom and pushed the gun and the ammunition under the bed and went downstairs.

The policeman was standing in the doorway. He was wearing a policeman's uniform but he was so short and square he looked more like a villain in a James Bond film.

–There's been a complaint,– Rose said, looking at me accusingly.

–A complaint?–

I thought about the gun upstairs.

–About the television.–

–The television?–

I looked over to the corner where Bangkok Rose's Mum was sitting with the telly on. I looked at the policeman.

–What's wrong with the telly then? We've paid our licence.–

For the first time the policeman spoke. You could have cut his accent with a knife.

–Ze complaint is from ze neighbours.–

I thought for a moment and then it dawned. –Oh no,–

I said, thinking of the workmen putting up the aerial and satellite dish on the roof.

–You've got the wrong crowd. This lot aren't Arab bombers. They aren't setting up a secret communications centre. This lot are Buddhists. They worship at the casino.–

I could see the copper's eyes flicking around trying to work out what was going on.

Rose's Mum didn't understand what was happening and had begun to flip through the channels trying to be helpful and show that we were innocent, when suddenly the copper shouted –STOP!– and we all froze.

He was pointing at the TV.

–Go back.– The accent was comic.

Rose's Mum flipped back a couple of channels and his face lit up. –It's Russian. You've got Russian TV!–

He turned to look at me. –I'm ze first Russian in ze Great British police force. I not see Russian TV for long time.–

In a minute he was sitting on the sofa translating the Moscow news for Rose's Mum, who by this time hadn't a clue what was going on but was smiling anyway. And I was thinking that upstairs under the bed I'd got a handgun and five hundred rounds of ammunition.

Then the Russian football results came up and Rose said –Would you like a cup of tea, officer?–

But this suddenly woke him up and he looked at his watch and said –No, no.– He was suddenly embarrassed. –No, no thank you.–

And a minute later Rose showed him to the door and he was gone.

I went straight back upstairs and packed the gun back into its box with the ammunition and put it in the cupboard under a pile of clothes.

That night I told Frank and he pulled a long face.

–We're going to have to do better than that Arthur. We don't want you hauled in by the coppers before we've got the operation off the ground.–

But the next day the policeman phoned to ask if he could come and watch the Russian news again that evening.

And Rose said yes, and he did.

And so that is how a week later I ended up taking Ivan the Russian down to the *Albert Arms* to meet the others.

* * *

We took the training for killing Billy Petersen very seriously.

When I did the recce I worked out exactly how many paces it was from the recess to the car and the angle at which Billy got into the back seat. Frank came with me one night and watched from McDonald's. Then we went back to the recess in daylight and measured out distances and angles properly.

–How much ammo did they give you Arthur?–

–They made a mistake. I asked for a box of fifty bullets, but they sent me five hundred.–

–Christ, you'll be able to start a war with all that lot.–

Frank got a picture of Billy leaning forward at just the right angle off the internet. Then he went to a copy shop and got five hundred copies printed up.

After that we had regular sessions on the Downs. To begin with it was hopeless. With the first few shots I missed altogether.

Frank said –You've got to learn to hate him Arthur.–

–No problem there Frank,– I replied.

–It's more than that. You've got to think of him as

sub-human, just a piece of meat on a butcher's slab. That's how the Japs did it on the Burma railway.–
Frank put me through a form of psychological training and soon I was happy to pump bullets into Billy all day long.

* * *

We didn't use the box again for a while after Dozey Dave ended up in Murmansk.
But then one day it was Nancy's birthday and we were wondering what to do and Smithy the Traveller said –Go to Hong King Jimmy's. Let the box order.–
So Nell got the menu and sat down with Stan and worked out a set of rules that would allow the box to choose.
–What do we do if it orders ten pairs of chopsticks and a flying carpet?– I said to Stan.
–Don't you worry Arthur,– he replied. –We've got it programmed.–
–Yeah, right.–
There was a crowd of us went in the end. There was Frank and Nancy, me and Rose, Smithy, Nell, Stan, Ivan and Ivan's Wife and Benny the Jeweller.
Hong Kong Jimmy eyed us up.
–What going on here Arthur? You want to order Chinese dinner or you want to play bingo with arsing box.–
You've got to know Hong Kong Jimmy. Some people think he's a miserable beef who should be sent back home to where he came from. He's got a face like an elephant's arse and he keeps a stick under the counter for whacking customers who get out of line.
One time he told Benny he was a high up beef in the Triads, but then Albert's Wife said she saw him and his wife on their knees in church.

–What you done with Dave?–

–Sent him to Russia.–

–Why you sent him to arsing Russia? He owe me money for horse bet.–

Jimmy looked at the box. –You take that arsing box out of here.–

He glared over at Ivan. –You arsing Russian. You got Dave hidden away somewhere?–

–Don't worry Jimmy. We're going to spend a fortune here tonight,– Frank said. –You'll be able to close up for a month.–

Jimmy gave a high pitched cackle, then glanced at Ivan. –You going to order arsing baked potato again?–

Sometimes it was difficult to tell the difference between Ivan and his wife. They were both small and square and dark. Ivan had mastered enough English to get in to the police force, but his wife thought she was still in Russia.

We could hear Jimmy on the phone in the back.

–That arsing *Hot Potato* takeaway?–

Pause for answer.

–Yeah well, this is arsing Chinese restaurant.–

Pause for cackle of laughter.

–Got to order potato for arsing customer. Arsing Russian can't eat Chinese food.–

He came back out to the front laughing and chuckling and rolling like an old sailor. You wondered how someone like that had ended up somewhere like here.

–Order baking potato for arsing Russian. Tell him deliver to Chinese. Bloke say stop arsing round. Says arsing hoax call. Say he not bring potato for arsing customer going to whack him round arse with arsing bamboo cane.–

Suddenly he stopped and looked at Ivan. –You still arsing communist or what?–

That stopped the conversation dead. Even Ivan's Wife looked up.

But Jimmy turned round chuckling and went back into the kitchen with his rolling gait.

Nancy rolled the dice for the first course and it came up Spring Rolls all round and we all relaxed.

The takeaway boy arrived with the baked potato for Ivan's Wife and we settled down for the evening.

The only problem was Stan. I could see he had his piece of paper out and he was yakking away to Nell.

–What's up Stan?– I said. –Seems like the box got it right.–

Mumble, mumble. Fag ash, fag ash.

Nell translated by saying that if there were ten people at the table and a choice of ten different starters the chances of everyone getting Spring Rolls were the same as Athletic signing Jesus Christ as its next striker.

Jimmy came out to clear away the plates. He was beaming.

–Arsing box got it right then. Chinese box, not Russian box.– He glared at Ivan and picked it up to examine it.

–It's made from camel bone,– said Benny the Jeweller. –Came from the desert in Africa.–

–Arsing camel bone.– Jimmy put the box down again.

–Only camel I ever saw was on race track.–

Haw haw haw.

–You going to ask arsing box to bring Dave back so I can whack him with bamboo cane?–

Then I rolled the dice for the next course and it came up Spring Rolls all round again.

Jimmy came out of the kitchen. He was angry now.

–I not the monkey's bum Arthur. This not arsing Spring Roll factory. You want to play game with arsing box you go down bingo. You keep ordering

Spring Rolls I going to report you to Racing Board for discrimination.–

Stan took his piece of paper from his pocket and consulted it and redid his calculations. I could see he was worried.

–It's statistically impossible,– he said.

He picked up the box and examined it and then passed it down the table to Benny.

The whole restaurant went quiet when we rolled the dice for the third time. This time the box didn't order Spring Rolls. Instead it ordered chocolate ice cream for everyone.

Jimmy just stared. Slowly and carefully he said –You want dump that arsing box Arthur. Going to cause you a lot of arsing trouble.–

Then he turned on his heel and walked away.

* * *

At the start I missed the target altogether.

–Christ Arthur,– Frank said. –You go on like that you're going to make an arse of yourself. Billy's going to think it's the Wild West with bullets flying everywhere.

In the end we agreed I only got one shot. We worked it out that if I took a pace forward I had just enough time to aim and get the shot off. At one point Frank played the bodyguard turning toward me. Then he put a stopwatch on me to make sure my timing was perfect. It became a simple move. Pace, brace, fire.

I got to the point where I could put a bullet into Billy's head seven times out of ten.

–Not bad, eh Frank,– I said one day after we had finished a session.

–But not good enough Arthur,– he replied. –You've got to be a hundred percent.–

* * *

One evening a week after the incident with the box at Hong Kong Jimmy's we were watching television when suddenly I burst out laughing.

Rose turned to look at me.

–It's not a comedy Arthur,– she said. –It's a serious documentary about the extinction of the Aborigines in Australia.–

–I know,– I said. –I'm not laughing at the telly. I was just thinking about Stephen Hawking.–

She turned to look at me.

–Who?–

–The White Coat. The case in the wheelchair who thinks he knows everything.–

–Oh, him.–

She still had one eye on the TV.

–What about him then?–

–If he'd been in the restaurant when the box began to order he would have fallen out of his wheelchair. His theory would have gone up the spout.–

–What theory?–

–His theory about the secret of the universe.–

She turned back to the television. –I wish he'd tell me the secret of this programme.–

–He says it's so complicated he's the only one who understands it.–

–Apparently the Aborigines follow ley lines. They're like motorways, except they're song lines.–

–He says it's either a worm hole or a black hole.–

–Or a bore hole.–

–A what?–

–A bore hole. That's what they have in Australia. It's where the Aborigines go to drink when they're following the ley lines.–

–Jesus, Rose,– I shouted. I was angry now. –I'm trying

to tell you that Hawking has got it wrong, that when he gets to the centre of the universe he's as likely to find Frank's magic box as a worm hole or a black hole or even a bore hole.–

Rose turned to gawp at me.

–You saw what the box did in the restaurant. There's no rational explanation for it.–

–You want to get out more Arthur.–

And so I did.

I went down to the *Albert Arms* to tell them my new theory. But when I got there I found Frank and Albert deep in discussion with a local sign writer.

On the table in front of them was a drawing of a familiar face with big ears.

Hassan the Syrian barman pulled me a pint and I joined them.

–I'm having a refurbishment,– Albert told me. –I'm giving the pub a new name.–

–Jesus Albert!– I was shocked. –Your dad will spin in his grave.–

Albert's Dad, also called Albert, had named the pub after himself. He was so conservative he kept the gas lamps for years rather than have electricity.

–The wife wants a change. She wants to get ahead of the crowd.–

Albert's Wife was always changing things. Every time you went in the tables were in different places. When she got really bad Albert said she even moved the plants in the garden. Nell said she was like a dog that couldn't settle.

–What are you going to call it?–

–The *King Charles*.–

I looked down at the drawing again.

–Right,– I said thoughtfully. –I see what you mean.–

* * *

We were divided by the performance of the box at Hong Kong Jimmy's.

Frank, Stan and Benny were against. They said they were businessmen and dealt in facts and not magic boxes.

Stan said –I can't explain it. But if I ran the betting shop using the box I'd be out of business tomorrow.–

Benny added –A twenty four carat diamond is always a twenty four carat diamond, it's never a bag of bananas.–

But Smithy said the box didn't go far enough. He said –I've seen medicine men in Brazil who can make your tongue come out of your arse!–

Rose was for. She said she liked the idea of the box ordering for her in a Chinese restaurant. –I like a bit of mystery. It's like a new dance or a song.–

I was with Rose. I said –I'm not a nutball. I don't believe in the Loch Ness Monster or the Archbishop of Canterbury or Father Christmas, but I am fed up with my life being run by business people and White Coats who think that *Krap U Luv* and *QuikSnooze* and villas in Spain are the way we should organise ourselves.–

I could see Benny and Frank and Stan looking at me but I didn't care. So I went on –I don't want to spend my life on my knees waiting to be carried up to heaven, but at the same time I don't want a White Coat like Stephen Hawking, who can't even get out of his chair to make a cup of tea, telling me he knows everything when he doesn't.–

–Arthur!–

–Don't Arthur me Rose,– I said. –That's what I think and that's all there is to say.–

And that was the end of the discussion.

* * *

In the end we solved the mystery of what Hemlock did with his money.

It happened when Rose's Mum was visiting from Thailand and there was a crowd watching TV.

It was yak, yak, yak and how much did you win at the casino and what do you fancy for dinner tonight, Indian or Chinese.

Then they'd channel hop till someone shouted stop and we'd have to watch the news from Vietnam or Bangkok or wherever. They even had Ivan's Wife in on it. Every so often she'd call out and we'd have to stop at a Russian channel.

Then Rose started telling the story of how Hemlock fed dog food to the residents in the home. They'd all had a few drinks and soon everyone was roaring with laughter.

Then suddenly this Chinese money in a short skirt sitting in the corner said –That sounds like Charles to me.–

So Rose turned to her and said –So who the chuffing hell is Charles then?–

The Chinese money was laughing fit to rip a zip.

–What does Hemlock look like?–

–Like a preacher who's lost his bible.–

–Tall?–

–As a chuffing tree.–

–Beard?–

–Yeah. We call him Miserable Christmas.–

Then the Chinese money said –Does he ever take a holiday?–

–Yeah. Three weeks. He's got a sister in Scotland or Cornwall or somewhere.–

–Twice a year?–

–Yeah. Regular as sewage. Chuffing hell. How do you know that then?–

So then the Chinese money gets herself under control

and says –When he comes on the ship he calls himself Charles. He's very pukka. Always the best dressed suit aboard.–

–Ship? What ship?– I said. –What's Hemlock doing then? Running a cross channel ferry?–

Then the Chinese money explained that she worked as a croupier on a cruise boat in Florida.

–There's a group of them,– she said. –They take the best suites on the boat. They're very rich, very discreet. They always have the best girls.–

–Jesus,– said Rose. –So Hemlock's got a girlfriend then?–

The Chinese money looked at her and said –No. Two.–

By this time the room had gone quiet. Even Rose's Mum had stopped chattering to Ivan's Wife.

–Two?–

–One Asian, one South American. Real beauties too. Model quality. Different ones for each cruise. All in the suite together.–

–Jesus.–

–Hemlock, you crafty old chuffer.–

–When we arrive at a port they all go off to the local casino together.–

–Who are the others in this group then?–

–Businessmen with money.–

The Chinese money leant forward. –One evening I was on the tables when Charles, sorry Hemlock, told me the story about the home owner who gave the dog biscuits to the residents. He said he'd read the story in the paper and that's why he finally left England. He didn't want to live in a country where people were so mean.–

–So where did he say he lived then?–

–Switzerland.–

–Jesus!–

Everyone sat back, stunned. They thought the story was over but I could see there was more. So I asked –What else is Hemlock up to then?–

The money turned to me and said –The film. The Deerhunter. Remember it?–

–Yeah. Vietnam. Robert de Niro.–

–The scene at the end.–

–Jesus!–

Rose turned to me.

–What is it Arthur?–

–Hemlock and his pals are playing Russian roulette.–

–Jesus.–

The Chinese money went on –It's when they get off. There might be a dozen of them in five or six cars.

–But when they come back they're always one short. They say he caught a plane or stayed on.–

I didn't sleep much that night, imagining Hemlock playing Russian roulette in the Caribbean when he was supposed to be visiting his sister in Cornwall or Scotland.

I said to Rose the next morning –A nutjob like that should be in jail. He shouldn't be running a care home. He needs sorting out.–

But Rose said –What's wrong? The residents are having the time of their lives and Hemlock is living out his fantasies.–

She could see I wasn't convinced. I wanted to get Smithy on the case. He was always banging on about greedy beefs who ran care homes forcing people to sell their houses so they could buy a new Porsche or a Rolls Royce.

But Rose wasn't letting up. She said –What are you against Arthur?–

–Mediocrity, *Krap U Luv,* people who don't stand up for themselves, bullies, abusers, takers, people who wreck my football club, aristocrats.–

–And what are you for?–

–People who've got the balls to do the right thing. People out there having a go, living on the edge.–

–Like Hemlock?–

I saw what she meant.

–Yeah, like chuffing Hemlock.–

So now I always breathe a sigh of relief when Rose tells me that Hemlock has returned safely from his latest visit to his sister in Scotland or Cornwall or wherever.

* * *

We had the final practise up on the Downs. We were working at night now with a lamp that Frank had rigged up to simulate the lamp over the door at the club.

Everything was in place. We set up Billy's picture at the correct angle to where I stood in the imaginary doorway. Between each shot Frank changed the picture in the frame and gave me a moment to recover.

At the end of twenty minutes I had put twenty bullets right into Billy's head.

Frank looked at me. –That's it Arthur,– he said.

–Yes,– I said and patted my stomach. –I reckon it is.–

* * *

One day Ivan beat up two men who were trying to rob Stan's betting shop.

–I whacked those nutjobs good and proper,– he told us that evening in the *Albert Arms*. –They not going to rob any more betting shops for a while now.–

There were four us. Me and Ivan, Stan and Nell. Stan was still shaken by what had happened.

–You must have thought you were done for Stan,– I said.

The two robbers had pointed their shotguns in his face.

–I've been in worse scrapes Arthur.–

–Yeah like what happened the day before,– said Nell.

Before she could tell us about that Ivan took over the story again.

–One of them gets a rabbit chop on the back of the neck and the other turns round and gets a broken nose.–

–Jesus Ivan you want to watch yourself.–

–Everyone says leave the police Ivan. Go private security. Make more money.–

–Was there anyone else in the shop?– I asked.

–Only Hemlock,– said Stan. –He was sitting in a corner trying to work out whether he was sixpence up or sixpence down. As soon as he saw there was trouble he scarpered.–

At this Ivan cut in again. –Yeah. Like ferret up hole. Arsey bastard.–

–Tell Arthur what happened to you the day before Stan,– Nell said. She turned to me. –That really scared him Arthur.–

But there was no stopping Ivan telling his story.

–So the cops finally come in with the stretcher guys. They say well done Ivan. You going to get medal for this. Need more guys like you on the Force.–

–He laid the pair of them out cold,– said Stan.

–So what the chuffing hell did happen the day before then?–

Nell answered for him. –His ex-wife came to visit!– Pause. –From South America!–˙

I looked at Stan.

–You're a dark horse Stan. You never told us about a South American ex-wife.–

Mumble, mumble, fag ash, fag ash. –It was a long time ago, Arthur. We got divorced.–

–She comes into the shop,– Nell said. –All skirts and perfume and says "Can I speak to Señor Stanley please?" So I said "And who is it who's asking for Señor Stanley?" And she said "Tell him it's his ex-wife!"–

Gawp, gawp.

–So I yell up the stairs to the back, "Stan, its your ex-wife, from South America!" "It's me what Nell?" "It's your former South American wife, you fat git. She wants to talk to you."

–Then I heard a window opening upstairs so I shouted up again. "It's no use going out the back Stanley. She's got that entrance covered too." I was almost wetting myself laughing.–

–I thought she was after my money,– Stan said.

Even Ivan had stopped to listen now.

–In the end it turned out to be alright,– Nell went on.

–She was on a package holiday from Venezuela and was looking up old friends.–

Mumble, mumble, fag ash, fag ash. –It was a long time ago. She was over here working in the casinos. After a bit we went back to South America together.–

–And what the chuffing hell did you do there Stan?–

–Bits and bobs, helping out. Ended up running a betting shop, same as here.–

–She had the family photos,– said Nell. –Latest hubby, latest children, latest grandchildren. Smart house, swimming pool. Looked like she's done all right to me. Better than this crummy place.–

–She invited me and Nell out there.–

I thought for a moment.

–None of the kids look like you Stan?– I said finally.

–Bit round in the face and with specs?–

He looked at me but said nothing.

–You tight chuff,– I told him finally. –You're just scared some little Stanley's going to climb out of the Amazon Basin and claim his inheritance. That's all you're worried about.–

Stan looked at me again.

–You're as tight as a duck's arse, Stan the Owl,– I said, and meant it.

After that I turned my back on him and spent the rest of the evening with Ivan discussing the merits of going into the private security business.

The gun went off and Billy and the bodyguard fell on top of me in a pile of blood and brains and piss.

–Fuck, fuck, fuck,– I heard the bodyguard yell. –Billy's been fucked.–

–Get off me,– I yelled back. –You're fucking suffocating me.–

He rolled off me but then he had me up against the wall and was kneeing me in the balls. After that I slumped to the ground again and was sick all over everywhere.

They must have a special code alert for people like Billy because half a dozen police cars arrived immediately, sirens blaring. Then I heard the bodyguard shout –He's dead, he's dead. Billy's dead, we're all dead, oh Jesus.–

After that two coppers cuffed my hands hard up behind me and put me in the back of the police car. They listened to the squawking and yelling on the radio for a minute and then we were speeding away from the scene.

When we arrived at the police station I knew straight away it wasn't a normal nick. It was more like a hospital ward. The lighting was subdued and it was deathly quiet. They put me in a cell and no one said a word, though every so often I could hear a noise and see an eye looking at me through the peephole.

We'd had an arrangement. My one phone call would be to Frank. I would say "The Eagle Has Landed," and he would alert Stan to come in and then ring Rose.

But there was none of that sort of nonsense allowed here. These were serious people who were trying to work out whether I was a terrorist or a nutjob.

They took me to an interview room where the door

opened and a tall thin beef came in. He was even more miserable looking than Hemlock. He sat down and stared straight at me hard without blinking. Then he got up and stood behind me and I could sense him sniffing me like a dog.

Finally he went to the door and I heard him say to the copper on guard in a low gravely voice –Get that arsehole out of my nick.–

And that was that. Within an hour I was out of there and in a proper police station, the sort you see on TV with beefy coppers and sour faced women.

* * *

The day after Billy's funeral my solicitor Lawrence Goose came to the prison to see me.

He looked serious. –Are you all right Arthur?–

–Never better thank you Lawrence.–

I could see him hesitating, so I said –If you're going to ask me if I regret whacking that nutball then the answer is still no.–

I could see he was exasperated.

Lawrence was very proper, very public school. He had taken over my case following the first visit from Stan the Owl.

–If the judge hears you talking like that he'll make a recommendation and you'll do another ten years.–

That got me angry. I had made my stand and I wasn't going to back off now, so I replied –He can stick his bloody black hat on and hang me if he wants. I don't care.–

I hadn't told him yet about the growth in my stomach that was killing me.

But there was no stopping Lawrence. He said –What about Mr Petersen's wife and children. Don't you feel anything?–

I leant forward and numbered the points off on my fingers.

–Did Churchill feel anything when he ordered the fire bombing of thousands of women and children in Germany? No.

–Did Thatcher feel anything when she ordered the drowning of hundreds of Argentinian sailors in the Falklands? No.

–Did Blair feel anything when he ordered the RAF to take the skin off the backs of the children in Iraq? No.–

I could see Lawrence was shocked.

–But that was war Arthur.–

–So is this Lawrence.–

–You should be careful what you say Arthur.–

–You know what makes me sick Lawrence?–

–I'm sure you're going to enlighten me.–

–Armistice Day.–

Lawrence looked pale.

–The old soldier sitting in the corner of the bar and someone saying, "It's thanks to you that we're not all speaking German," and somebody else adding, "Hanging's too good for Polianski." It's all so bloody unfair.–

He was staring at me blankly now, so I changed tack.

–Do you ever see the Tour de France on television?–

–No.–

–Well, you've missed out. Lance Armstrong is one of my heroes. He's supposed to be in his grave with ten types of cancer but he's out there stuffing it to the French instead.–

–Where is this taking us Arthur?–

I leaned over the table towards him.

–At the beginning the riders set off in a pack. Then one of them, like Lance, breaks away. To begin with the pack lets him go, but then they chase after him and pull him back.

–But they've got to judge it just right. Because if he gets too far ahead, they'll never be able to reach him.–

I stopped and looked up.

–That was the problem with Billy. He'd got too far ahead. The pack couldn't pull him back.

–In the end he had more money than half a dozen African countries put together. He was sitting at home pissing himself laughing.–

Then I remembered something Smithy the Traveller had said. I repeated it to Lawrence. –Every day some poor case opens up *Tombola* and wishes he was dead. Every day some arsehole of a traffic warden, some gobshite of a solicitor, some social worker with pork scratchings for brains has their lives mashed to a pulp to feed *Tombola's* insanity.–

I stopped and stared at him.

–Yes, I do understand all that Arthur,– he said finally. –But I still don't see that you can go round shooting people just like that. You just can't do it.–

He still didn't understand.

–Billy was the one that got away Lawrence. He was the wild dog. He was outside the law. And I was the only one who had the guts to hunt him down. All you cowards did was sit at home and pretend it wasn't happening.–

Still there was no response.

So I said –What do you like to do Lawrence?–

–Do?–

–Yes. Do. You know. Hobbies, sports, that sort of thing.–

–Well, I'm captain of my golf club.–

I stopped and thought for a moment and then I said –Let's pretend the Wherever Golf Club is the social centre for the Goose family. Lawrence is the captain. Mrs Goose is on the committee. The little Gooses have their birthday parties there. Great grandfather Goose was a founder member.

–And then one day a hot-shot developer comes along and buys up the Wherever Golf Club. There are protests and appeals. But the hot-shot developer has got more money than the Wherever Golf Club. He's got more money than the Goose family. He's got more money than the local council.

–And the hot-shot developer is not going to turn the Wherever Golf Club into a nice comfy holiday camp. Oh no! The hot-shot developer is going to turn it into a refugee camp for ASYLUM SEEKERS.

–And not nice ordinary comfy asylum seekers from Europe, but asylum seekers from Africa.

–And not nice ordinary comfy asylum seekers from Africa, but asylum seekers with dongers THIS BIG.–

I held out my arms wide and Lawrence moved back quickly.

–And what's going to happen to the price of the nearby Goose family residence when all this happens Lawrence?

–It's going to drop down to zilch, zero, nothing, not even a bean, not even a nice round ladies bum. In the end you won't even be able to give the Goose residence away.–

I looked straight at him.

–And what are you going to do to stop all that happening Lawrence?–

He thought for a moment and then said, with a snarl in his voice –Shoot the fucker!–

I leaned across and clasped his hand.

–Thank you Lawrence. At last. Thank you, thank you.–

* * *

I had the same argument with Oliver Gosling who was my barrister.

I liked Oliver. He was a cut glass toff, but he had something about him.

Lawrence said he was reckless.

–He bets on the horses and takes on hopeless cases.–

–Thank you Lawrence,– I said.

–No offence Arthur.–

–None taken Lawrence.–

I said to Oliver –The General was right to invade Iraq. All the gobshite liberals parading around like arses make me sick. When somebody starts feeding people feet first into the office shredder you've got to whack them. You've got no choice.–

I was warming to my theme now. –And here's my point Oliver. If the General can put down a wild dog like Saddam, why can't I put down a wild dog like Billy Petersen? Where's the difference? Answer me that if you can.–

But he couldn't.

Another time when we were discussing my case Oliver said I should plead insanity.

–Lie doggo and tell them what they want to hear and you'll be out in ten years.–

–No thanks Oliver,– I replied. –I don't want some teenage White Coat filling me up with drugs and telling me I'm the bastard son of the General.–

After that I told Oliver and Lawrence that I was dying.

I could see they were shocked.

Oliver shook me by the hand and said –Got the full picture now, old boy. In your shoes I would have done the same thing.–

One day I said to Oliver –Mind if I ask you a question Oliver?–

–Fire away, old boy.–

–Do you ever shop at *Krap U Luv?*–

–Certainly not, old boy. Wouldn't dream of it.–

–Good for you.–

I didn't ask Lawrence the same question.

I reckon you could divide the world into two halves. Those who shopped at *Krap U Luv* and those who didn't.

* * *

As my case wound its way through the courts I was more convinced than ever that I had been right to whack Billy.

I'd admitted right from the start that I'd done it. I told them all I wanted was my day in court to say why. But that didn't stop them dragging me through hearing after hearing.

And every session of wig tugging and harrumphing and legalling was another down payment on a villa in Spain for someone.

When it had been going on for some time I began to notice things.

There was no doubt we were two different races. In the jail we were a miserable species, coughing and spluttering, bronchial and asthmatic and wheezing and complaining and either pigeon chested or so fat we had to bend down to see our knobs. We were complaining and illiterate and ignorant and hopeless.

But in court it was a different world. The judges and barristers had been living off the fat of the land for generations. They were smooth and pampered and perfumed and their skins were as sleek and shiny as lizards.

One day when I was on remand they brought an old bloke in to my cell. The first thing he did was sit down on his bunk and burst into tears.

–What's up?– I said. –Forgot your toothbrush?–

–They've sent me down for fiddling the social.–

I could see he was in shock.

–But it's not just me. They've sent my wife down as well. She's crippled. She's supposed to have a new hip next month.–

–Oh Christ,– I said, and went over to the window to let him sort himself out in peace.

I told Oliver Gosling about it the next time I saw him.

–What's going on Oliver?– I said. –Someone whacks an old girl behind a Post Office counter, he deserves to get banged up. But this is just plain wrong.–

Oliver nodded his head.

–Everyone knows that judge,– he said. –He thinks he's still at school thrashing the lower orders. But he'll have to watch himself from now on.–

–Oh yeah. And how's that then?–

–The plods caught him in a public lavatory with an African boy. It's all been hushed up but he's been told if it happens again he's out.–

–Oh Christ.–

It takes a lot for me to agree with the French. But I reckon they got it right with their revolution. We should haul this lot off to the guillotine and start again with a fresh sheet.

For a while we had that judge on my case.

He'd look at me over the top of his glasses as if he were picking out a pork chop at the butcher's and wondering whether he wanted me grilled or fried.

A couple of times I wanted to stand up and say that I knew what he was up to, that he was putting his knob up an African boy in a public toilet, but Oliver gave me a look and I shut up.

It was the injustice of it all that made me want to scream.

If I could have changed places I would have reached for the black hat and said –I sentence you, Sir Gerald Hard Arse or Sir Bertie Long Cock or Lord Bere Splodge, to death by hanging for the crime of taking more than your share, for forgetting that we inhabit this planet the same as you.–

Then one day Oliver came in and said –Bit of good news Arthur, old boy.–

–What's that Oliver, old boy.–

–Judge has dropped dead. One too many gins in his club and over he went.–

–Well thank God for that,– I replied. –Break open the champagne.–

For Oliver and Lawrence it was double good news. The case went back to square one, so they could reset the meter and start all over again.

* * *

When all the harrumphing and wig tugging and play acting was over Oliver Gosling stood up. –Messrs Gosling and Goose for the defence your honour.–

I had to hide my face behind my hands. Then I peered round and saw that Rose and Frank in the gallery had their heads down as well, trying not to laugh. Then the judge looked round like the head in assembly working out who had been scraping their chair on the floor.

Oliver Gosling had arranged it so I could speak before I was sentenced. He said not to go on too long, but I reckoned I was allowed a go before I was sent down.

I had the indictment all typed up and ready in my pocket. We had all the facts and figures, as dug up by Nell and Stan and Smithy and Frank. We had Billy Petersen trussed up like a pig.

Then it was my turn and I stood up and everything changed. Suddenly I didn't want to give Billy any more publicity. Suddenly I was fed up with Billy. Suddenly I cared as much about him as I did about a slab of meat on a butcher's counter.

I took a deep breath, put my notes back in my pocket, glanced at the evil case in the horse hair wig in front of me, and started to talk about what Athletic meant to us all.

I told them about the day we went to Wembley and how Frank scored the winning goal in the final minute and how the celebration was too much for his dad and how he died in a nursing home six months later.

I told them how Nell got us to all the matches on time and how she knew more about train timetables than the train companies themselves.

I told them how Albert the Landlord had to ban Smithy the Traveller from the *Albert Arms* pub quiz because he always knew all the answers. And how as a result we had put him in for Mastermind on TV, but that the day he was supposed to go on he forgot all about it and went off to South America to investigate a silver mine instead.

I stopped for a moment. I was going to tell them that I was on my way out too.

I looked over to the table where the Ratcatchers sat. Their heads were suddenly up, noses sniffing the air, scenting something big coming up.

So I said to myself no, I'm not going to give those bastards the pleasure.

So instead I told them how I used to mark out the pitch with Jack the Gateman. And how after we'd finished Jack would go in goal and I'd knock penalties past him and turn to the empty stand, raising my hand in the air like a Roman Emperor and imagining what it would be like to hear ten thousand people roar my name.

I told them how every Saturday afternoon was an adventure.

I told them of the season when the half time pies had so much meat in them that when you bit into them the gravy spilled down the sides of your mouth. I told them how you got back to your seat after half time, the taste of the pie still in your mouth, and the team would be trotting out and you'd shout down –Get stuck in Frank!–

And he'd turn and give you the thumbs up and you knew he was going to do it.

And you'd roar them on until you were hoarse. And they'd batter away at the opposition with Frank leading the line until five minutes from the end there'd be a corner and Frank would go up and smack the ball home into the top corner of the net with his head, and you'd go OOOOOAAAAHHHH.

We weren't Spurs, we weren't Arsenal, we weren't Man U ...

I looked at the judge. Then I looked at the Rat-catchers scribbling in their notebooks and I said –It was our club, your honour. It was our home. It was our life. And Billy Petersen was going to take it away from us.–

I sat down and looked around. The judge and the barristers looked at me as if I'd been describing life on Mars. Underneath all the flammery they were hard bastards. They'd have understood the balance sheet on Billy's life better. But then I looked up at the gallery and saw all the gang up there and I could see their eyes were red with tears and I knew that I'd got it right.

* * *

–But where is it all going to stop?– The judge was looking down at me. –You have already shot poor Mr Petersen. Now who else are you going to shoot Mr Polianski? Are you going to shoot your greengrocer if he overcharges you for his apples? Are you going to shoot your butcher if you are dissatisfied with his meat? No, no, Mr Poliank013i. This won't do, this won't do at all.–

And with that he leaned forward and said simply –I sentence you to life imprisonment.– Just like that.

When they take you down they want you to be terrified. They want you to think that you're being taken into the underworld to be tortured forever. That's what it's all about. It's a piece of theatre put on by the evil gobshite in the horse hair wig.

But I didn't feel bad at all. I went back to the cell and tucked in to the pie and chips they brought me for my lunch and thought that I had done a good morning's work.

I don't know what the normal procedure is in prisons, but this lot let everyone in to see me.

Frank came in and hugged me and said it was the best speech he'd ever heard in his life.

Nell didn't say anything. She just hugged me hard and didn't budge an inch when I held her bum with both hands.

Smithy shook me by the hand. I could see he was shaken. Then he looked at me and said –Arthur Polianski, you are my hero. I salute you.–

After that they all came in, Stan, Ivan, Benny. They even let Albert the Landlord from the pub in.

–Christ Albert,– I said. –I feel like I'm on This Is Your Life.–

Finally Rose came in. We hugged each other. Then I held her face and said –I'll always love you for ever Rose.–

And she replied –I'll always love you for ever too Arthur.–

And that was that. The door slammed shut and they were gone and suddenly I was alone.

* * *

Frank told me later that the TV news had filmed me being taken out in a convoy of trucks with camera lights flashing.

In the van I could hear the guards talking. One of them had been at the match when Athletic had won the Terrier's Dog Food Cup.

–Good luck to the bloke,– I heard him say. –About time somebody nutted Billy.–

I watched the motorway and the cars and the fields speed by us. Half way there I had a twinge in my stomach.

Rose had said –Why don't we pretend it's a baby and call it Billy.–

As we turned off the motorway up toward the prison the sun began to set. Another day had passed and Billy was growing bigger and stronger and more confident inside me. I patted my stomach and leant back and closed my eyes.

Prison is like living on the worst housing estate in the world. They don't put you in here because you forgot to pay your library fine.

No. They put you in here because you rented your children out to the local child molester so you could have a night out in the pub with your mates.

Or because you cracked your granny's nut open with a meat cleaver so you could steal her pension book to buy drugs.

Or (most likely) because you smell and you're fat and you can't read and you can't write and you keeping putting your knob into places where it isn't supposed to be.

People in prison are out of control. They're driving with both feet on the accelerator and with the brake wires cut.

A beef comes toward you on the wing and you don't know if he wants to share a cigarette and have a yak or if he wants to throttle you because he thinks you're from the planet Uranus.

But it was easier for me than for most of them.

If you've murdered your wife or run over a baby or robbed a pension fund of a million pounds so all the workers are left to starve you probably feel like shite. But I didn't feel like that. Not at all. I was a hero. I'd whacked Billy Petersen. I'd done my bit to make the world a better place.

I also knew that the life sentence I was supposed to serve was unlikely to be more than a year.

* * *

It's funny the way things work out.

I said to Frank on a visit –Guess who's on my wing Frank.–

–Who's that Arthur? Frank Sinatra? Bing Crosby? Cliff Richard?–

–No. A Moroccan case who chainsawed a beef's head off in a drugs scam.–

–Oh yeah?–

–He's called Mohammed. I told him about the camel bone box. How you bought it in Morocco. How it did all sorts of daft things. He agrees with me. He says its got magical properties.–

–He's a drug dealer and a murderer Arthur.–

–He says it was made from camel bone by the Touareg. They're the tribe who live in the Sahara desert. He says they're well known for producing things with magical properties.–

–What's he going to do then? Whisk you out of here on a magic carpet?–

–He's got this music as well.–

–Is this another musical obsession Arthur?–

–It's the music the Touareg play. It's like two banjos talking to each other. Like the Burt Reynolds film. He plays it all the time. It's hypnotic. It gets right inside you.–

There was a silence after that, so I said –So how's Rose then? Is she still upset?–

–Not now. She's got over it.–

Billy's Ratcatchers had found she was claiming on the social to top up her wages from Hemlock's care home when she wasn't supposed to be. The council took her to court and now she's got to pay it all back.

* * *

When you're in prison you yak a lot. You tell stories. Sometimes they're true and sometimes they're not. But you don't call someone a lying nutjob unless you want to get nutted yourself. You just nod your head and say right, right.

So one afternoon when Mo told me he'd started out as a dog handler in the Moroccan police I didn't say a word. Everyone knew he was a drug dealer who'd cut off a beef's head with a chainsaw.

I could see him looking at me. –I can get a dog to do anything. I can whistle a command you won't even hear.–

I couldn't resist that so I said –Can you whistle up a couple of pork chops for our tea tonight then?–

–You'll see man,– he said. And I did.

A week later we were standing on our chairs in our cells looking out of the window. The One Eyed Scotch Bastard was standing at the far side of the yard by the wire, yakking to one of the other screws. Directly below us was a dog handler with his dog. For a moment he'd taken his hand off the dog's collar to get at a flea or something on its neck.

Suddenly I heard Mo say from the next door cell –Watch this Arthur.–

I heard him give a faint high pitched whistle which made me want to rub my ears as if something had irritated them.

The dog had heard it as well. Its ears pricked up and it looked up towards the cell block. Then it ripped itself away from the handler and launched itself across the yard straight towards the One Eyed Scotch Bastard.

Before the handler could move the dog had its nose up the One Eyed Scotch Bastard's backside and his balls in its mouth. Then there was a piercing scream and everyone who was watching from the cell block gave a cheer as the One Eyed Scotch Bastard went down with the dog on top of him.

The dog handler lost his head completely. –NUT THE

FUCKING DOG,– he yelled at the second screw. –NUT THE FUCKING DOG BEFORE IT FUCKING KILLS HIM.–

Eventually the pair of them managed to wrestle the dog off, leaving the One Eyed Scotch Bastard with his arse exposed to the wind and the dog with half his pants in its mouth.

A hundred men at their cell windows cheered and shouted and made monkey noises as two other screws came out with a stretcher and hauled the One Eyed Scotch Bastard out of the yard.

The long term cons said it was the biggest victory since they'd ripped the slates off the roof in the riots twenty years ago.

But you had to be careful. Every wing had a grass. I waited till association and just touched Mo on the shoulder and said –Well done Brother.–

The One Eyed Scotch Bastard was off for a month. When he came back he walked with a limp and the prisoners taunted him about how his Mrs wasn't getting any. You could see him getting more wound up about it by the day.

Over time screws develop a sixth sense. It could be that someone grassed on Mo, but it was more likely that the One Eyed Scotch Bastard just sniffed it out.

One night I was in my cell when I heard a commotion from Mo's cell next door. I heard Mo cry out. It was obvious he was getting a beating. I jammed my bell and eventually a screw came.

–Mo's getting a beating,– I said.

–Go back to sleep Arthur,– the screw replied. –It's personal, none of your business.–

Next morning Mo had a couple of shiners and a broken nose. But he still had a twinkle in his eye. Mo had had worse beatings than that in his time.

–Reckon I got a result there Arthur.–

–Reckon you did Mo.–

I switched on the radio one morning. The whole cell lit up with the JOY OF SPRING. I couldn't wait till the screws opened up so I could tell Mo.

–I've done it Mo.–

–Done what Arthur?– Mo sounded gloomy.

When you're doing life with a recommendation of at least thirty years because you've cut a beef's head off with a chainsaw it's not always easy to look on the bright side.

–I've stopped them.–

Blank.

–Stopped who Arthur?–

–It's just been on the radio. *Tombola's* pulled out of the deal to rip down the ground. Athletic's saved.–

His face lit up. –Well done Brother!–

Mo always called me Brother. I think he wanted me to convert to Islam.

The word soon got round the wing and people were congratulating me, even the screws. Everyone knew that Billy had been a nutjob and that we had been very wronged when he tried to wreck our club.

I heard one of the screws say to another –They should give that bloke a medal rather than banging him up in here.–

* * *

I got on well with Gerald the Irish Screw. Some of the screws would do you a bad turn if they could, but Gerald was the opposite.

One day he told me that he had a daughter back home in Ireland who'd been turned over by a Rat-catcher there.

–He came sniffing round the house one evening. In

the end we had to call the police to have him put out. It was only a few kids messing with old cars, but he made out it was a load of big shots terrorising everyone. My wife was in pieces over it. So when you whacked Billy, I thought good for you, getting our own back like.–

One afternoon I was sitting in my cell when he came in.

–You're getting fat Arthur,– he said.

Little did he know what was growing inside me.

–I'm not going to the gym or anything like that,– I said, –but I'll join an art class if you like.–

Gerald replied –It'll do you good to get out of your cell.–

So I went.

I even persuaded Mo to come with me. We had become good friends by this time. We spent hours yakking together about life in the desert.

He had a brother who owned a factory in Casablanca making jeans. He said you could make a fortune smuggling the jeans into Algeria on camels.

We sat in his cell listening to the Touareg banjo music and discussing the details. You had to get it right. Mo explained what the Algerian Border Guard would do to you if they caught you.

Then one of the screws started taking an interest in us. He probably thought we were plotting a breakout, so we had to pack in our chats. As a lifer you get an easier ride than the other prisoners, but you don't want to push it too far. You've got to respect the rules.

But we still had the music. No one was bothered about that unless they thought we were going to fly out of the place on a magic carpet.

I got stuck in to the art class. I remembered what a miserable bastard Van Gogh had been and how he had never sold a painting in his lifetime. That put us half on level pegging. I wasn't a miserable bastard, but I had certainly never sold a painting.

I hated Whingeing Howard the teacher right from the start. He was a Welshman with long hair who was always complaining he was hard done by because he had to look after his wife who was in a wheelchair. He looked down on the cons as well.

I also hated him because as a painter he was hopeless. His water colours were so much watered down piss. I couldn't believe he'd been to art school.

Then one night I was lying on my bunk thinking of the desert and how we were going to get past the Algerian Border Guard when it came to me in a flash. I wanted to bang on the wall and shout through to Mo, but he wouldn't get it and it would only upset the screws.

But at the next art lesson I persuaded Howard to let me have a go with oils.

I put the yellow of the desert down immediately. Then it was squiggle, squiggle for the camels and finally dashes of blue for the turbans of the Touareg tribesman.

I stopped and looked. I'd been going so fast I was sweating. Then I turned the figures of the Touaregs into blocks and placed them geometrically and at angles to each other and I knew I had it.

Just a glance at the painting and you heard the rhythm and form of the music.

Mo glanced over and grinned when he saw it. He understood straight off.

–Hey Brother, you got it right. That's just how they are.–

Of course that alerted Whingeing Howard who just couldn't keep his long nose out and came grumbling over.

He grabbed the painting from my easel and showed it round to the other cons, who sniggered.

–Word of warning to you Arthur. Anyone taking the piss in my class gets their arse kicked. Alright?–

I could see a screw looking in through the window to see what the raised voices were for, so I let it drop.

He and I both knew that picture was something he could never have produced in a hundred years. That's why he was so pissed off.

But there was an odd end to my career as a prison artist.

It was a Sunday morning when Gerald the Irish Screw came into my cell with the Sunday edition of *Tombola.*

–What's up Gerald?–

–You're famous again Arthur.–

–Christ, what have I done this time?–

He showed me an inside page with my art class painting prominently displayed.

–Bloody hell Gerald, how the hell did that get there.–

But of course we both knew the answer. Whingeing Howard had sold it to one of Billy's Ratcatchers.

I read the headline out loud. Gerald was almost wetting himself laughing.

NOW BILLY PETERSEN'S KILLER IS MAD ARTIST.

–Jesus, Gerald,– I said. –There should be a law against that sort of thing.–

In the story some psychiatrist had written that the painting showed I was so dangerous I would certainly kill again if I was ever let out.

Everyone else thought it was funny. I was the only one who was pissed off. I went to the art class the following week just to spite Howard, but the weak kneed nutjob wouldn't look me in the face.

But there was an even stranger conclusion to the story the following week.

One of the posher papers printed the picture as well. But this is what they wrote:

ORIGINAL PRISON ART
By Rorie A Smith

A painting produced in prison by Arthur Polianski, the killer of Billy Petersen, proprietor of *Anglo-Norwegian* and the publisher of *Tombola* is a revelation.

Mr Polianski has captured perfectly the light and shade of the shifting desert landscape.

But more importantly and almost unbelievably for a beginner, he has also captured in the figures of the Touareg tribesmen their haunting rhythmic desert music ...

And so on, and so on ...

Now was that strange or not? The case could see right inside my head!

* * *

Mo moved with the other Muslims in the prison and he had strong political views.

–You pissed all over us in Africa, Arthur.–

–I've never even been near the place Mo.–

–You, the Belgians, the French ...–

I cut in. I was angry now. –Hold on,– I said. –Even the General can't do anything with the French Mo.–

But before I could say anything more he was off again.

It was us, we, me, the French, the Belgians, the Germans. Even the poor bloody Portuguese copped it. There's no doubt we'd acted like arses. But by the time I'd heard how the Belgians cut everyone's arms off in the Congo I'd had enough.

–You can go on all night,– I said, –but your lot haven't acted that well either.–

That stopped him. So I went on –What about that case with the Leopard Skin Hat who stole all the oil money?–

He was still staring at me.

–You've got to sort yourselves out and look to the future Mo.–

That set him off again.

–THE FUTURE! You pinched everything we ever had Arthur. And you're still at it. Nothing's changed. All we've got left is …– He stopped and looked round the cell before rounding on me again. –All we've got left is AIDS and poverty and starvation and a GENERAL FUCKING MESS.–

That was too much for me. I shouted back –You keep buggering each other up the arse Mo, the result is you get AIDS. It's as simple as …–

But before I could finish he had me by the throat and up against the wall at the side of the cell.

–For Christ's sake Mo,– I said, pulling myself away and shaking my head. –I'm on your side. I'm the case that whacked Billy, remember? The big fat capitalist who's been screwing you over for generations. I'm a hero. You should be giving me the Leopard Skin Hat, not banging me round the chuffing cell.–

–Sorry Arthur, you just rattled my cage a bit there.–

–Yeah, well, right.–

Then I remembered what Albert the Landlord had said, that a lot of people were better off when we were in charge over there.

I watched Mo take a deep breath and wondered if I was going to be thrown round the cell again.

Finally he said –Personally I'd rather be a free man

on an empty stomach than a prisoner with a full belly.–

I looked round the cell. We were well enough fed. We didn't have anything to worry about. We could laze about all day. But there wasn't one of us that wouldn't swap that to walk out of here and take his chances again in the outside world.

–I know what you mean Mo,– I said. –You've got a point there mate.–

* * *

When the pain got too much Gerald got me in to the see the M.O. He tapped and banged and said I had to go to the hospital for tests.

–Are you going to keep the chains on when I see the doc?– I said to the One Eyed Scotch Bastard as we walked in through the main door of the hospital.

People were staring at us. One or two were nudging and pointing.

–Can't have you jumping on any of those nice nurses now can we Arthur?– his oppo replied.

The doc was as good as gold. He made no reference to the fact that I was chained to a couple of goons who wouldn't know an X-ray from a sunray.

–There's a couple more tests I would like to do before you go Mr Polianski.–

Mr Polianski! There was no doubt he was doing it deliberately to wind the screws up. I was enjoying it, but I didn't want the doc to go too far. I didn't want to get back to the prison and find some screw had pissed in my tea. You had to be careful like that.

In the end we were there half the afternoon.

I wondered, what does a screw say to his wife when he gets home at night?

Does he say –Bloody brilliant day dear. Led a man

round on a piece of string like a dog in a circus.– Or does he say –Hand me a rope. I think I'll just hang myself before dinner.–

They got upset when a nurse came in and smiled at me and then went out again. Word had got out who they had in the hospital that afternoon.

When I got back I told Mo all about it. He said it was a real victory. He was going on and on, so in the end I had to say –Hold on a minute Mo. It wasn't a day at the races. They had me chained up like a wild animal while the doc worked out how long I have before I die.– That made him go quiet.

That night I lay on my bunk and thought about dying. I wasn't scared at all. I'd gone through all that when the doctor told me in the first place. In the end you had to look at it as giving you a chance to leave your mark. I would go down in history. And that was no exaggeration.

Me, Arthur Polianski, who sold photocopiers, would go down in the history of the world!

I couldn't resist it. I went up to my window and hauled myself up and shouted –ARTHUR POLIANSKI YOU'RE A HERO.–

I grinned when Mo shouted back –No you're not Arthur, you're a waste of good prison space. Go back to sleep.–

I was going to shout back again but I could hear a screw starting to pad down the corridor toward us.

But I slept well that night, the best for months, with no pain at all.

* * *

The end of the world came a week later. Gerald the Irish Screw was walking along the wing handing out the mail.

–Good news for you Arthur,– he said as he gave me a letter. The screws always read the letters before they were handed out.
I sat down on my bunk and opened the envelope from the hospital.

Dear Mr Polianski,
Blah de blah de blah de FUCKING WHAT!
... misdiagnosis ... nothing wrong with me ... symptoms probably hysterical reaction due to situation I found myself in ...

The words went blurred. My brain froze.
THE SITUATION I FOUND MYSELF IN! I had made a total arse of myself.
Instead of being mourned a hero I was facing twenty years in this place. I would come out a vegetable. Everyone would be wetting themselves laughing.
I looked up to see the One Eyed Scotch Bastard standing in the doorway.
–Bit of bad news Arthur?–
His face split into a grin. I was in shock. I just stared at him, my mouth open. There was nothing I could say.
–Monkey lost his bollocks has he?–
And he went off down the wing whistling.

* * *

One day three months after I got the news that I wasn't dying I woke up. I don't mean that I had been asleep all that time. I had simply become a zombie.
–A lot of the men get like that,– Gerald the Irish Screw said. –Especially if they've just been turned down on appeal. They go in on themselves. The mind takes time to adjust.–

–That's right,– I said. –It certainly does.–

–I used to come in and find you just sitting on your bed staring. You had a terrible temper on you if you were disturbed. The governor wanted to send you to Broadmoor.–

I shivered at the thought of it.

–Thanks for keeping the faith Gerald.–

–Not at all Arthur, I knew you were alright really.–

I worked out what I had been doing. I had been counting. Counting the paint spots on the walls. Counting the flecks of dust on the windows. Counting the strands of material in the mattress. I'd get angry when someone came into the cell and disturbed me because it meant I had to go back to the beginning and start counting all over again.

Eventually, when they thought I was ready, they gave me a job in the kitchens. So that was how I rejoined the human race, scouring pots and peeling spuds in a prison kitchen.

Then one day, when I was in my cell, I began to laugh. I said to myself –You should be dead by now Arthur.–

But I wasn't. I was alive. So I was seeing things I shouldn't be seeing. Suddenly every day seemed important.

I agreed that Rose could come up on a visit.

–It's good to see you Arthur.–

–You too Rose.–

She looked awful but I didn't say anything. She'd dyed her hair blonde and put on weight. Normally I'd have told her to get her arse down to the gym and then move right on to the hairdresser.

But no words came out of my mouth. So we just sat and looked at each other.

Finally I said –Been dancing down at the *Trocadero* then?–

More than anything I would have liked to have been on that dance floor with her.

–No. Not at all.–

–Mexican Pete still there?–

–No. He cleared off. Took all his gear.–

At the end of the visit I said –Love you Rose.–

–Love you too Arthur.–

Tears welled up in both our eyes and I knew it would be OK.

* * *

I adjusted to life in prison. What was happening inside became more important than what was happening outside. A change in our food or a new prisoner being transferred on to our wing was a major event in our lives.

And I spent more time yakking with Mohammed about life in Morocco than I did talking to Rose or Frank or the others.

After a while I began to see visits as intrusions. There were times when a visit was scheduled and I'd panic and try to call it off.

I'd say to Gerald the Irish Screw –Cancel my visit Gerald. It only upsets me. I've got plenty of things to do here.–

But Gerald, I'd give that case a medal any day, would reply –No. Come on Arthur. You can't give up. You've got to keep the contact.–

And so I went.

Over the months they all came. Rose, Frank, Smithy, Nell, Stan the Owl. Even Hong Kong Jimmy was going to come until he got cold feet at the last minute.

As Frank said –He's scared that once they get him in here they won't let him out again.–

Instead he made up a special giant spring roll called a Billywhacker and put it on the menu in honour of me.

I lay on my bed and thought of him bringing the Billywhacker out to Frank and Nancy and Stan and the rest of them.

–Special arsing spring roll. Special for Arthur. Big enough to put arsing file in.–

Haw haw haw.

* * *

I got a letter from Frank to say that Athletic were naming a new stand after me! That cheered me up more than anything. A new crowd had taken over the club. Frank thought there was even a chance we might get back in the League.

That night I looked at myself in the mirror and said –You're a chuffing hero. You're the man who saved his football club.–

I began to take a pride in myself. I went to the gym and started to shave every morning. Frank's news about Athletic and Rose's first visit were turning points for me.

One day Gerald the Irish Screw said –You should take a course. A lot of men do. You could get a degree.–

–Oh yeah, right!– I replied. –I'm the bloke who left school without a GCSE to his name. Remember?–

–You never know, in ten years time you could be a rocket scientist.–

–Yeah and blow the lid off this chuffing place.–

We both laughed at that. Gerald was a good man. Along with Mo I counted him as my only true friend in this God forsaken place.

* * *

Stan came up one time with Nell.

Mumble, mumble, fag ash, fag ash.

–What's he saying Nell?–

–He's saying you're a hero in Venezuela.–

–In where?–

–In Venezuela. In South America.–

–In Venezuela? I've never been to Venezuela in my life.–

–Stan's ex-wife wrote to him. She says there's a bloke in Venezuela who Billywhacked a tycoon after he cut his workers wages.–

–Jesus. What did they do to the case?–

–They took him to court, but when he told them that the tycoon had ruined his life they let him off. He said he had been following the example of someone called Arthur Polianski in England.–

–Bloody hell, Nell. I hope the tycoon deserved it.–

–Must have. Stan's ex-wife says the Billywhacker's so popular he's going to run for president.–

–For President? Jesus. Didn't I ever pick the wrong country.–

I looked round the squalid visiting room. There wasn't one of us that wasn't spluttering or wheezing. There was one con who was so fat he had to pay his cell mate to tie up his shoe laces for him.

Lying on my bed in my cell that night I thought about the story from Venezuela.

I didn't want people using my name to settle a score. As I'd said to Lawrence Goose and Oliver Gosling, the whole situation was as rare as hen's teeth and what I did was a one off.

And there were plenty of times when I woke up in the middle of the night sweating, thinking I'd made the most terrible mistake in the history of the world.

So I said to Nell the next time she came up –I don't want this chuffing business turning into a cult, Nell.

I don't want to end up nailed to a cross like Jesus Christ.–

I could see her looking at me strangely. Then she said –I don't think we need to worry too much about that Arthur.–

The next time she came she had more detail about the tycoon who'd been Billywhacked in Venezuela.

–He was a real nutjob. The workers organised a strike and he had the leaders shot. After that he robbed the pension fund and went off on a cruise with a Chinese money.–

–That's all right then,– I said, feeling relieved.

* * *

Nell began to look at me in a strange way on her visits.

I said to Frank –What's going on with Nell. The way she's looking at me, given half a chance she'd be over the table and sitting in my lap.–

Frank laughed. –You're a desperado Arthur. All women love a desperado. She can't stop talking about you. If you'd gone armed robbing ten years ago you'd have been in her pants just like that.–

–What does Rose say about it all?–

–Rose is about ready to chin her.–

I sat back and laughed. –Fighting over the body eh?–

* * *

Another time Nell came up with Smithy.

–Where you been then Smithy?–

–Blackpool.–

–Blackpool? Chuffing hell, Smithy, you're certainly slipping. Whatever happened to Niagara Falls and Timbuktoo?–

–I threw the dice in Frank's box.–

I started to laugh. –I always knew that box had a sense of humour. It was Dozey Dave who was supposed to end up in Blackpool, not you.–

–Blackpool's a dangerous place,– said Nell.

–Oh yeah, how's that?–

–He fell off his donkey and bruised his head.–

I told the story to Mo that night. He nearly wet himself laughing. But then he warned –You want to watch yourself with that box Arthur, it'll get you into trouble one day.–

* * *

Ivan and his wife came up in their security guard uniforms. They were jet black with a blood red snarling dog insignia on each shoulder. I could see by the way the screws looked at them that they were impressed.

–Business good then Ivan?–

–No more arsing criminals in my parish, Arthur.–

Alongside his Russian English, Ivan had now added half digested police English as well as phrases from Hong Kong Jimmy's colourful vocabulary.

I could see him looking round at the cons in the visiting room.

–Boys on the Force begging me to go back.–

Frank had told me that Ivan now provided security for all the local businesses, including the *Albert Arms* and the betting shop.

–Going to bring some of the boys over from Russia. Nice bit of muscle there. Can start to clean up neighbouring parishes as well.–

–What do you do with the criminals you catch Ivan?–

The pair of them leaned back and cracked their knuckles as if they were doing a bizarre musical duet. Then Ivan leaned forward. –Let's just say they're not troubling Her Maj in here. Know what I mean Arthur?–

Haw haw haw.

He was even beginning to laugh like Hong Kong Jimmy.

* * *

One day Rose came to visit me looking very down in the mouth.

–What's wrong with you Rose? You'd think it was you locked up in here, not me.–

I'd just finished a workout in the gym and the adrenalin was pumping round my body.

–It's Hemlock,– she replied. –He hasn't come back from his holidays.–

–Jesus. Have you phoned his sister?–

–Don't be daft.–

–Yeah. Right.–

We talked about other things. The new crowd had taken over at Athletic and work was starting on the new stand that was going to be named after me. But I kept thinking of Hemlock.

–Does anyone else at the home know where he goes?–

–No. Just you and me.–

I imagined Hemlock's body being heaved over the side of the dock in some sweaty South American seaport. –Bye, bye, gringo. Go sleep with the fishes,– or whatever they say on those occasions. If only they could have seen him here, trundling along on his bike, tight as a duck's arse.

–Maybe that Chinese money was just spinning a yarn,– I said hopefully. –You never know, he might really be at his sister's in Cornwall or Scotland and just got held up.–

–So why didn't he ring?–

–Yeah, you're right.–

A few days later I rang Rose and she said Hemlock had turned up with a bandage round his head and a story that he'd been in a car accident.

I told Mo about it that night and he laughed. –Best thing I ever heard, Bro. Chuffing nutjob can't even put a gun to his head.–

But the brush with death left Hemlock a changed man. Rose said –Last week he gave the residents a party, telling them his sister in Cornwall or Scotland had died leaving him her money.–

–Do you know if he's planning any more cruises?–

Rose laughed. –I hope not. I hope the bang on his head has brought him to his senses.–

* * *

I used to yak a lot with Gerald the Irish Screw. He told me about life in Ireland and I told him about Athletic and so on.

But Mo used to say –Be careful there Bro. Never trust a screw. If you get too close people will think you're a grass.–

And one day I had a reminder that Mo was right, that all screws, even if they could be helpful at times, were bullies at heart.

It happened when a big beef with a short temper chinned a screw in a row over a visit.

I stepped out of my cell and saw that half a dozen screws, including Gerald the Irish Screw and the One Eyed Scotch Bastard, had the beef down and were kicking and punching him.

When they'd finished they came back up on the landing and I could see that Gerald was as wide eyed and excited as the rest of them.

After that Gerald kept out of my way for a while, until one day he stood in my cell door and said –There are different ways of doing your time Arthur.–

I looked up. I was still wary after what I had seen on the wing. The beef who had got beaten up was still in the hospital.

–What do you mean Gerald?– I said.

He hesitated. –If you invite me in I'll explain to you.–

–Alright.–

So he came in and when he had got himself comfortable he said –When I was at school with the Christian Brothers in Ireland I learned two things. The first was how to take a beating without shouting out and the second was how to do time.–

–Go on.–

–It was one of the Brothers. He said there were different sorts of time.– He stopped and looked around. –For instance, how many steps are there down off this landing Arthur?–

I thought. –Twenty, thirty?–

–And how long does it take you to get down them?–

I thought again. –Twenty seconds. Less if I'm quick.–

–And when are you due to go down them next?–

–When I go to collect my lunch.–

Then he looked at me and said –When you go down them try to concentrate. Be aware of everything you see, feel and hear as you walk down. Don't think about anything else.–

I wanted to laugh. I'd never seen Gerald serious like that before, but I kept a straight face. I said –Sounds easy enough.–

–We'll see.–

In the end I lasted five steps before my mind began to wander. But Gerald kept on, he was a good teacher.

After a week I could get right down to the bottom of the steps without my mind wandering. I could hear the sound my shoes made. I could see the light reflecting off the metal handrail.

I began to look forward to going down the stairs. It became an important part of my day.

Then Gerald said that as I lay in bed at night I should go back over the ascents and descents of the stairs during the day. And then in the morning I had to preview going down to collect my meal tray at lunchtime.

–It's like a video,– he said. –You play it over and over. Stop, pause, rewind, fast forward, slow motion, whatever you want.–

Soon I realised that I was creating a new sort of time. As I went backwards and forwards I saw things I had missed originally. I was filling in detail that I had missed the first time.

Soon I was able to use Gerald's system to enrich my whole day. I also began to use it to replay incidents in my life before I had come into jail. It was like looking at an old black and white film and being able to turn it into colour.

I went back to the Terrier's Dog Food Cup Final at Wembley. I saw the pens in John Motson's shirt pocket. I smelled the perfume Nell was wearing. I even saw shots on goal I had missed before.

I told Mo about it. He was suspicious. –He's hypnotising you Bro. Sounds like a trick to me.–

–No Mo,– I replied. –You're wrong. It's simple. It's just that you need a place like prison to sort out a technique like this.–

As the months went by it began to control my day. It began to make prison not only bearable but at times enjoyable. I watched everything and used the different types of time to flesh out my life.

The system was another step on the road to recovery, to my coming back from the dead.

One day Gerald said –So what do you think then Arthur?–

I replied –I think you're a chuffing time traveller Gerald, a chuffing Irish time traveller. That's what I think.–

He laughed. –It's all thanks to the Christian Brothers, Arthur.–

–And I'll certainly thank them personally when I get out Gerald.–

We both laughed at that.

* * *

I lay on the bed in my cell and using the system Gerald the Irish Screw had taught me replayed Athletic's victory in the Terrier's Dog Food Cup Final at Wembley. The trouble started when I replayed Frank's winning goal.

I watched the corner come over. The ball hung. Frank climbed. I stopped and sat up quickly, feeling the sweat on my forehead. Then I lay down again. I replayed it over again. The ball came over. It hung. Frank climbed. Frank climbed! Climbed! Frank had climbed! I could see it now. I sat up again. He was on the shoulder of one of their centre backs. It had all been pre-planned. Two of our players were deliberately shielding him from the linesman and the ref.

Then I remembered what Frank had said the week before the game. –We've got a secret move planned Arthur.–

–What's that then Frank?–

–Wait and see.–

Well I certainly saw now.

Getting up I slammed my hand against the cell wall as hard as I could.

–Mo! Mo!–

–What is it Brother?–

–It's Frank, Mo, it's Frank. He cheated. He climbed on the defender's shoulder. That's how he scored the winning goal at Wembley.–

Pause. –Go back to sleep Arthur. You're having a bad dream.–

I could hear a screw padding down the wing to see what all the noise was about, so I let it go and slumped back on to my bed.

But I couldn't sleep. I couldn't sleep because I was angry.

Next time Frank came on a visit I came straight out with it. –I know what you've been up to Frank.–

–What's that Arthur?–

He looked as guilty as hell. I wondered if he'd been seeing more of Rose than he should have. I knew he'd always fancied her.

–You cheated at Wembley in the final.–

–You what?–

–I went through it again. You climbed up on the defender's shoulder. You had it all planned.–

I could see him looking at me.

–So what if we did Arthur,– he said finally. –We won didn't we? That's what you wanted wasn't it?–

–But we didn't win fair and square.–

–What the hell are you on about Arthur?– He was angry now. –We were out there to win the chuffing cup.–

–But we should have won it fair and square Frank.–

–Jesus, Arthur. Put it down to the hand of God. Maradona style.–

–No Frank. No. It wasn't the hand of God. It wasn't any of that South American nonsense. It was eleven

Englishmen out on that pitch playing for something I gave my life for.–

I knew what he was going to say next. I knew Frank.

–You mean something Billy Petersen gave his life for Arthur.–

I didn't say anything after that. I just signalled to the screw to take me back to my cell.

It was true what they were saying. Prison was driving me crazy.

* * *

As soon as the beef who had chinned the screw could walk again he was shipped out to another jail. In fact Mo reckoned he'd set the whole thing up so he could get a transfer.

Some cons were so desperate to move they'd do anything. I was the opposite. I had my routine and I was happy enough sticking to it.

Then one day Gerald the Irish Screw came to my door and said –Fancy a little holiday Arthur?–

I looked up from the book I was reading.

–Yeah, why not Gerald? They say New York's nice this time of year.–

–I'm serious Arthur. A little break down by the seaside. Get some fresh air.–

He explained that they were looking for cons like me, ones with a reputation, to go to a south coast jail for a couple of weeks to be poked and prodded by a group of White Coats holding a conference. They wanted to find out what made desperados like us commit our unspeakable crimes.

–Why don't you ask Mo,– I said. –He cut off a beef's head with a chainsaw.–

–So you won't go?–

–No arsing way.–

But then I woke up in the middle of the night and thought why not? It was only a couple of weeks and the break would do me good.

So two weeks later Mo and I found ourselves in the back of a prison van heading towards the south coast. They put us in separate compartments in the van and kept the cuffs on, because we were desperados going to a desperados conference, but I didn't mind.

It was a sunny day and I watched the countryside speed by. Using the method Gerald had taught me I absorbed everything. I heard the hum of the engine and the murmur of the screws' voices coming from the front.

Then suddenly there was a THUMP and a BANG and a CRASH, and for a moment everything went pitch black. Suddenly I realised we had crashed and that the van was on its side and the door was open and I could step outside.

I was standing in the road eyeing the wreckage of the prison van and wondering what I was going to do next when I heard Mo and this other case shouting at me from the back of a red Peugeot.

–Don't stand there like an arse, Arthur, we haven't got all day.–

I ran over to the car and Mo opened the rear door and I got in. They had keys to get my cuffs off. There were two other Arab looking cases in the front.

–Who's this Mohammed?– the driver asked as he gunned the motor and we sped out on to the road. I could see him giving me the evil eye in the rear view mirror. For a moment I thought I'd rather take my chances with the screws.

–This is Arthur,– Mo said. –He's all right. He's the bloke who whacked Billy Petersen.–

The driver's face lit up. –You that bloke? You did a good job there Brother. You want a smoke?–

The car was full of the acrid aroma of hashish.

–No thanks,– I said looking out of the window.

I turned to Mo. –You had this planned for a long time Mo?–

–Yeah Arthur. This is my brother.– He pointed to the driver. –He owns the jeans factory in Casablanca. We all going back there.–

I groaned. –Jesus Mo. We've just wrecked a prison van. There's screws lying all over the road. They're going to get us for this.–

–Be cool man.– He took another long drag at the cigarette and passed it to the case in the passenger seat. –Be cool man. Everything going to be cool.–

I looked down at my filthy prison clothes.

When we were far enough outside any area the police would have cordoned off, I spotted a phone box in a lay-by and told them to pull in. Then I borrowed a handful of change from the gangster in the front passenger seat and got out.

I looked back in through the window and saw Mo's grinning face swathed in hashish smoke.

–You're a case Mo, you really are,– I said. –But I hope you make it anyway.–

–Inshallah, Arthur. Inshallah. Don't forget. See you in Morocco.–

–Yeah, right. Here's hoping. Inshallah Mo.–

With that he wound up the window and the car pulled away and I was left to trudge over to the phone box thinking how I'd been dropped in the shite once again.

* * *

With my back to the road I dialled Frank's number.

–Frank?–

–Yeah.–

–Listen. It's me.–

–How's it going Arthur?–

–Unbelievable. I'm out. Now don't say anything. Just do as I tell you.–

A minute later I slipped out of the phone box and into a thicket of bushes to wait.

Two hours later Frank's white van dipped its lights and pulled in to the lay-by.

Looking this way and that and seeing no one I nipped out. Frank leaned over and opened the door and I jumped in.

–Questions later Frank,– I said climbing into the back. –Just get the chuffing hell away from this place for now. There are probably coppers everywhere.–

Frank put the van into gear and pulled out on to the road again. Quickly I scrabbled out of the prison clothes and put on the ones he had brought me.

Half an hour later when it was dark I got into the front passenger seat. For the first time I began to relax.

–There's some pies and bits and pieces in a bag at your feet that Nancy sorted out.–

–Thanks Frank.– I bit into a pie, feeling the grease and the fat and the richness of the meat.

When I'd finished I looked at Frank. He was still my friend. I had got over my anger toward him for cheating in the Terrier's Dog Food Cup Final. I started to laugh.

–I've done it Frank. I can't believe it. I've busted out of jail.–

–Yes you have, you certainly have Arthur,– he replied thoughtfully.

After that we sat in silence.

Frank turned the radio on and we were top billing on the news.

We were a gang of dangerous stop-at-nothing desperados and the public were warned to keep clear of us. We were armed and dangerous.

–Chuffing hell.– I said. –The way they're going on you'd think I had an atomic bomb stuffed down the front of my pants.–

I turned to Frank. –Did you do as I asked?–

–What's that Arthur?–

–The cash, my passport. I've got to get out of the country.–

Silence.

–Bit of a problem there Arthur.–

–Problem?– I could feel myself getting angry. –What problem Frank? It couldn't be more simple. I asked you to go round home, pick up my passport, get the stash of money from under the bath and tell Rose to meet us. We drive down to Dover, I hide in the back under the matting and Bob's your Uncle we're in

Calais and twelve hours later I'm in the sunshine in Spain. What could be simpler than that?–

–That's the problem. Rose wasn't expecting you out so early Arthur. She had a bit of a clear out.–

–A CLEAR OUT!–

–Christ, Arthur, you got sent down for life. You're supposed to be dead of a tumour. You're not even supposed to be here.–

–Where's my passport Frank?–

–She binned it along with the rest of your stuff. She's really sorry Arthur.–

–And the money?–

–She had to live Arthur. There's some of it left.–

–SOME OF IT!– I yelled. –I've only been gone about five minutes. There was thousands under the bath.–

–Yeah well.–

Suddenly it all fell apart. I looked at the road signs. Bristol, Taunton. –Where are we going Frank? This isn't the way to Dover.–

Silence. –We're going to Cornwall, Arthur.–

–Cornwall? What do I want to go to fucking Cornwall for? I hate fucking Cornwall. This is the usual fucking disaster. Take me back to the nick Frank. I've had enough already.–

–Smithy's Mum's got a place down there. Very secluded. No one's ever going to find you there. Rose is going to come down soon.–

* * *

Several hours later we arrived on a cliff top in Cornwall and Frank pulled the van in to the side of the road.

I rolled down the window and poked my head out into the pitch black night and smelled the sharp nip from the sea air.

I groaned and closed my eyes. All I wanted was to be back in my nice warm prison cell.

–It's the end of the chuffing world Frank.–

But Frank was already out of the van and going down the path. Soon all I could see in the dark was the pin point light of his torch.

Five minutes later we were standing in front of a small wooden chalet and Frank was fumbling for the key. I shivered, listening to the sound of the sea on the shore below. The wind was blasting against us.

–This is like a bad film Frank,– I said as he finally got the door open. –We're the desperados hiding out in the wilderness.–

–You haven't seen anything yet Arthur. The wind gets up here you have to tie yourself down with a chain.–

He flicked the torch round the inside of the chalet. I picked out a table, a couple of chairs and a gas cooker.

–Jesus, Frank. My cell's better than this.–

Frank lit a gas lamp and the light flickered round.

–There's a gas heater over there. That'll keep you warm.–

In another room at the back there was a bed with a sleeping bag on it.

Frank opened the box on the table.

–Smithy's Mum has done you alright for food.–

Five minutes later Frank was gone. He said he had to get home before anyone missed him.

–I'll be back with Rose when the coast is clear.–

I sat on the chair looking at the red glow from the gas fire and listening to the hiss from the flare of the gas light. I could hear the sea below.

In the nick we'd be banged up now and I'd be reading my book. I'd hear noises that were familiar. Maybe there'd be a shout and a screw would pad down the wing to sort it out. Then I'd put my book down and switch on the radio.

There'd be times during the evening when I'd look at the door and wish I could open it and walk out on to the wing, but the point was you knew what was happening, you knew where you were when you were inside.

I looked at the door for a long time. Then I got up and went to the window and peered out, but there was nothing to see. Then I opened the box of groceries Smithy's Mum had left. I found a packet of sandwiches which I opened and ate without sitting down.

After that I went through to the other room and by the light of the torch surveyed my sleeping quarters. I made myself a cup of tea. Then finally I got up the courage to open the door and step outside.

* * *

I sat on the bench outside the chalet and looked out over the sea and thought of the panic there would be back in the prison. The screws would be on edge, anyone who stepped out of line would get a smack. The only one I felt sorry for was Gerald the Irish Screw. He was my mate, he had looked after me. I hoped they wouldn't take it out on him.

The moon came out from behind the clouds and I could see the silver of the sea way below me. The wind on my face was cold and clean after the fetid air of prison. I started to laugh. Then I stood up and shouted at the top of my voice into the wind –I'M ARTHUR POLIANSKI. I'VE BROKEN OUT OF JAIL AND I'M A DESPERADO AND I DON'T GIVE A DAMN.–

After that I got up and went back inside and shut the door behind me. I got into my sleeping bag and went to sleep, waking when the sun was well up and there was a knocking on the window. A woman with long straggly hair was peering in.

–I know who you are,– I said as I let her in. She put down a pile of papers on the table and I saw my picture on the front page of *Tombola.*

–You're Smithy's Mum. You're the spitting image.–

She gave me a hug and then stepped back and looked at me. –Every inch a hero,– she said.

She even had Smithy's voice.

* * *

I had a lot of time to think on the beach. During the day I'd lie on my bed and read or stare out of the window. At night I'd prowl along the beach, occasionally dipping my toe into the water and staring up at the stars.

I wanted to pass a message to Rose to tell her not to come down. I couldn't see how she could have thrown my passport away and spent all that money.

I said to Smithy's Mum –It's not right what she did. What was the cow thinking of?–

–She wasn't expecting you out love, that's all,– she replied, dragging on a cigarette. –You were supposed to be dead or banged up for twenty years. She was getting on with her life, that's all.–

She stubbed out her cigarette. –I wouldn't ask where the money went if I was you. I'd let it rest.–

I thought about it for a moment and then said –You're right.–

And that was that. And anyhow I'd left another stash of cash with Frank just in case.

One day *Tombola* had an interview with one of the screws in the prison.

–Listen to this,– I said to Smithy's Mum and quoted

from the paper. – "Billy Petersen's killer is a dangerous stop-at-nothing. He's killed once and he'll kill again. Every time I looked into his eyes I could tell he was evil."–

–That'll be the One Eyed Scotch Bastard,– I said. –Give him a couple of pints and he'll say anything.–

Tombola had also reprinted the picture I had painted of the Touareg tribesmen in the desert. And again they'd got a psychiatrist to say it proved I was a dangerous desperado who would certainly kill again. Whenever they had a story about me they always printed the police station mug shot they'd taken when I was first arrested.

I said to Smithy's Mum as we were having a cup of tea –That picture is going to be a problem. Right now the only person in the country that's better known than me is the Queen.–

* * *

Eventually Rose and Frank turned up. Frank said –We had to go halfway to Scotland to make sure we weren't followed.–

Rose dumped a load of bags on the floor.

I gave her a hug and said –Good to see you Rose.–

–You too Arthur.–

I could see she was nervous. Frank would have told her that I was angry and that she was going to get her arse kicked. But I didn't say anything because I'd listened to what Smithy's Mum had said and because I was glad to see her anyway.

* * *

Frank, who had always fancied himself as a writer, had been busy feeding false information to the papers. One day *Tombola* had a report that I had gone to Morocco with Mo.

They called me African Arthur and said I planned to flood Britain with super strength cannabis that would drive people mad. Apparently my price for springing Mo from jail was that he would cut me in on his evil drug empire in Morocco.

Rose was going to be my chief lieutenant, organising a string of poor African women to act as drug mules.

A Ratcatcher had taken a picture of her leaving *Krap U Luv* with her shopping, and it had been printed next to mine.

After that they had a story saying that prison officers had searched my cell after the escape and had found evidence that I planned to Billywhack the King of Morocco.

"As an experienced assassin, it is believed that Polianski could break through the security cordon that surrounds the monarch to deliver a fatal blow to him."

I looked up at Frank. –That your work Frank?–

–A few taps of the keyboard, old boy.–

–You should have been a writer,– I said. –You're a chuffing genius.–

Then one day *Tombola* announced that they were offering a million pound reward to anyone who brought me in.

–That's more than most, isn't it Frank?–

–How do you mean Arthur?–

–Well most rewards for desperados are lower than that aren't they, usually about five thousand?–

Frank looked at me and laughed.

–Don't get big headed Arthur. The papers never actually pay the money out. It's only talk.–

* * *

I looked in the mirror.

Rose was giving my hair a different cut and dying it lighter. Frank had given me a pair of glasses with plain glass in. After that they said I should grow a moustache and that would be enough.

–Come off it,– I said as they worked. –Anyone will spot me straight off. It'll be You're Arthur Polianski And I Claim My Reward.–

But Rose and Frank had it all worked out.

–How many people do you know Arthur?– Frank asked.

–Know? How do you mean Frank?–

–How many people, if you met them on the street, would say "Hello Arthur, nice to see you?"– Rose explained.

–Right, I see. I don't know. Twenty, fifty?–

–And what's the odds of any of them bumping in to you down here on the beach?–

–Thousand to one?–

–And how many people would recognise you from your picture in the paper?–

I looked down at the face in the *Tombola* picture, a snarling rat caught in the light of a police flash gun.

–Half the bloody population of the country.–

–And the chances of bumping into one of them down here?–

–A hundred per cent. It's going to happen.–

–So what you really look like doesn't matter. All we have to do is make sure that you don't look anything like the picture in the paper.–

–Right, I see,– I said thoughtfully.

I looked at myself in the mirror. They were right on both counts. Anyone who knew me would see through the disguise straight away. But there was no way I looked anything like the face in the paper.

I checked in the mirror again.

–Swedish or Danish?–
–Or maybe Norwegian?–
We all laughed.

* * *

On the beach we became George and Lisa. We'd sold our business and we were planning our next move.

Winter gave way to spring and we were able to sit outside on the bench and look down on to the beach and the sea. The smell of sand and sea and wild flowers became part of our lives and for the time being I forgot all about prison and being on the run.

Then Frank came down with the news that because of the story in *Tombola* that we planned to Billy-whack the King of Morocco we were being hunted there too.

–They've thrown a ring of steel around the King,– he said. He was even beginning to speak like one of his stories. –They flash your pictures up on the screen every night.–

–Thanks for nothing Frank.–

I was getting fed up with his stories. So a week later he told *Tombola* that we had moved to Portugal and were going in to the timeshare business.

–That's better,– I told him.

After what Mo had told me I didn't fancy a Moroccan jail.

* * *

One day Rose said we had a visitor who was going to stay for a while.

–Who's that Rose?– I asked, surprised.

–You'll see.–

An hour later she came down the cliff path with her

mum trailing behind her. She gave me that wide gap-toothed grin. I wanted to say what the hell are you doing here you crazy old bag of wind but instead I put my arms around her and said –Good to see you Rose's Mum.–

–Good to see you too Arthur.– She reached out and felt my biceps. –You big guy now. Professional hit man.–

–Yeah, well, maybe.–

–I on the run again too.–

–The Cambodian hit man?–

–Yeah. But this time he serious.–

I lay in bed that night listening to Rose and her mum yakking away in the front room. Then I went to sleep and dreamed that the cops and the Cambodian hit man were fighting it out on the cliff top.

At breakfast Rose said –Mum wants you to come to Bangkok. Run the *Bloods Head* bar for her.–

Rose's Mum looked at me. –You important guy now Arthur,– she said. –You killer, you busted out of jail, you on the run too.–

–Right,– I said, finishing my tea and getting up to look out over the bay. –Give me a moment, I'll think about it.–

In the end Rose's Mum settled in fine. If there was a prize for the best Thai cook living in Cornwall on the run from a Cambodian hit man she would win it.

–You should write a recipe book,– I said. –You would make a fortune. Then you wouldn't have to run a bar any more.–

–But I no good with writing Arthur. You come work for me in Bangkok, you write all down for me.–

There was something about Rose's Mum. In many ways she was a chuffing idiot, but then you thought if everyone was like her the world would be a better place than it is today.

One day the pair of them decided to go in to Plymouth to the casino. I said fine we'll all take the bus. –No, no,– said Rose. –Mum doesn't go on buses.–
–Why not?–
–I've ordered a taxi.–
–A taxi? We're supposed to be desperados in the middle of nowhere and you're ordering taxis?–
One night they even ordered a taxi back out from the city centre to the cliff at three o'clock in the morning.
I said to Rose over breakfast –I'm surprised that didn't make the front page of *Tombola* by itself.–

* * *

We made friends with our neighbours in the other wooden chalets on the cliff. There was Leo the Artist and then there was Titus.
–Where did you get a name like Titus?–
–In the Navy. They called me that because I used to get on everyone's tits.–
You could see that. He'd stand there cricking his neck. He still had a trace of ginger hair, though he was near enough bald. In winter he wore a sheepskin coat and a pork pie hat.
Rose said –Titus always looks as if he's about to burst out of his chuffing skin.–
You could say to Smithy the Traveller –What time is it on the moon?– And he'd reply –Twenty past four,– or whatever.
But if you said something like that to Titus he'd just stand there cricking his neck, staring at you with his great eyes bulging, trying to work out if you were taking the piss.
After we'd known Titus a few weeks we realised we had an unexpected romance on our hands.

I'd say to Rose –Where's your mum?–

And she'd reply –Down at Titus's.–

And we'd give each other a knowing look.

–You know he hasn't got a bean,– I said.

–He told mum he's got his naval pension.–

–Oh Christ, that's it then, now we'll never get rid of her.–

–Arthur!–

–Just make sure she's divorced from the last one, or we'll have more than the Cambodian hit man to deal with.–

I wondered what the Cambodian hit man would make of Titus. They would probably bore each other to death.

Titus was always hammering and fixing his house. I'd go down to say hello and I'd hear all the banging, but I wouldn't be able to work out where it was coming from so I'd go inside and suddenly Titus would pop his head up from under the floorboards or from round a corner. –Alright Arthur?–

–Alright Titus?–

And I'd ask him what he was up to and I'd get an answer that droned on for half an hour, making me wish I hadn't asked in the first place.

After a while I started painting again. But I'd lost the edge I'd had in prison and I ended up with a series of drippy sea scenes. Howard the Whinger would have liked them, but I knew they were no good. They were bromide in the tea stuff, no cojones.

If Van Gogh had been at the centre of a happy family circle instead of being a social outcast he would have given up painting and taken up gardening or DIY.

It was the same with the time travel technique that Gerald the Irish Screw had taught me. I still used it. It still enriched my day, but it didn't have the same power it had in the prison.

I was happy with Rose down on the beach and I was getting fat and lazy.

Then one day Titus came up to the house. He picked up a canvas I'd done and looked at it and then put it down.

–Don't say anything, Titus. I know it's hopeless.–

I could see him thinking.

–Why don't you paint the night sky Arthur?–

–Give over Titus.–

–I'm serious.–

So that's when we learned that there was nothing about the night sky and the stars that Titus didn't know.

He'd come up night after night during the fine summer weather and we'd sit outside the house on the bench or lie on our backs and he'd tell us everything about the stars.

He knew all the stories. He knew every star up there in the sky. His voice changed when he talked. He lost that awful drone he normally had.

–Does anyone live up there then Titus?– Rose asked one night.

–Oh yeah,– he replied confidently. –No doubt about it.–

One time on a visit Frank had made me a present of the magic box. I think he was trying to make up for everything that had happened with Rose spending all the money and me catching him out cheating in the Terrier's Dog Food Cup Final.

To pass the time we developed the game further and Titus tried to help, but his ideas were all over the place.

I'd ask a question like –What are we going to do if they roll a three and a five?–

And he'd stop and think and say –Send 'em to Buenos Aires or Montevideo.–

But then one day Leo the Artist told us –Titus was a sailor on one of the ships that was sunk by the Argentinians off the Falklands. He got a bang on the head and spent hours in the water covered in oil.–

Which explained why sometimes he didn't seem to be living on the same planet as the rest of us.

I did some night sky scenes, using the reflection of the moon on the water, but Rose said –They're still flat Arthur, like you're not really interested.–

Rose did better than me. With Titus's help she started making jewellery using patterns from the night sky. Titus picked out the shapes and images for her. The one I liked best was one she made out of shells and pieces of wood that she'd found on the beach. It was an image of Venus sitting above a crescent moon.

* * *

One night we had a great storm on the cliff.

We'd invited Titus and Leo for dinner and after we'd eaten we played cribbage. But the wind started to rise and Leo said he wanted to get back.

In the middle of the night I woke up suddenly. Rose was awake beside me. We'd both heard a noise above the sound of the wind and the rain.

Then we both said at once –Titus!–

So we struggled into our clothes and went down the cliff path to find Titus holding down the roof of his house, which had broken loose in the storm.

We got ropes attached and held on until the worst of the storm had passed.

But by that time we were all exhausted and soaked through and Titus came up to spend the night with us.

I was standing in the front room drying myself when I heard Rose starting to laugh. I turned and saw

Titus giving me a strange look. Then Rose took me into the bathroom and said –Look at yourself in the mirror Arthur!–

And I did. –Jesus Christ,– I said.

In the storm I'd lost my glasses and the dye in my hair had started to run so that the old Arthur Polianski was starting to re-emerge. And because I was in such a state I looked a dead ringer for the prison photos of me that had been handed out to the Rat-catchers.

So Rose told me to stay in the bathroom while she got Titus settled down on the settee and then came back and helped me re-dye my hair and find my spare specs.

In the morning I could see Titus looking at me. At one point he opened his mouth to say something but then shut it and said nothing.

* * *

–Oliver Gosling here.–

–Oliver, it's me. Arthur Polianski.–

–Arthur you scoundrel. Don't tell me where you are.–

–It begins with M.– I said, looking at the cover of the phonebook where someone had scrawled Mousehole Girls Do It For Nuffing. He roared with laughter.

–Lawrence and I toasted your escape. Many congrat-ulations.–

–Thank you Oliver.–

–The judge was furious. He says if he catches you he's going to cut your balls off.–

I laughed.

–Good to hear you Arthur. Love to Rose. Don't call again.–

* * *

The managers at the casino hated Titus. They hated him because they couldn't work him out. Most people came to the casino to play on the tables, though they might have a wife or a money who would stay at the bar or wander round looking at the other tables, or watch the TV in the corner.

But Titus just stood behind Bangkok Rose's Mum as she played blackjack and watched.

The managers are always on the lookout in a casino. If they think you've got a fiddle going they'll have you out.

But they couldn't see inside Titus's brain. They couldn't see that the bang on the head he'd got in the Falklands had altered his memory so he remembered everything.

He counted the cards as they came out of the shoe. Then he gave Rose's Mum a signal if there was going to be a run of high or low cards so she could alter her betting.

As a result the percentages moved in Rose's Mum's favour, and she won more than she lost.

The managers knew Titus was on a scam. They were just waiting for him to make one wrong move and they would throw him out.

Then one day something happened which changed everyone's view of Titus.

We were sitting outside. The sun was shining on the empty beach below us. It was one of those days when it was difficult to believe that I was a dangerous desperado on the run.

Rose said to me –Why don't you come in with us this evening. Nobody'll know you.–

So I did. Titus drove us in. Rose and I were in the back and Rose's Mum was in the front next to Titus. When we got to the casino Titus took up his normal position behind Rose's Mum at the blackjack table.

I ordered a drink at the bar and looked over to the tables. I could see that Titus was uneasy.

He had started to hunch up his shoulders and sway slightly from side to side, a sure sign he was unhappy. Then he started glancing toward the roulette table on his left.

I said to Rose –Something's up there.–

Rose knew the way casinos worked, so she explained that a group of Chinese were on a scam.

–A crowd on the far roulette table is distracting the pit boss while a crowd on the near table is hustling the croupier who's new.

–When she puts the marker down they crowd her so she doesn't see they're moving pieces on to the square after the spin.–

–Where's the manager?– I asked.

–In his office smoking a cigar, where he always is.–

We watched Titus to see what he would do. He was getting more and more agitated. He was hunching his shoulders and moving from side to side. Finally he snapped and turned and marched over to the table. Then he picked up two of the Chinese gamblers by their collars and carried them, dangling like a couple of pups, to the door.

–Jesus,– said Rose. –Look at him.–

The whole place ground to a halt. Even the Chinese lost their gobs. Everyone was gawping at Titus carrying the gamblers to the door. We watched as he butted the door open with his head and dumped them outside. Then he walked back to the blackjack table and resumed his position, all without saying a word.

Even Rose's Mum turned to stare at him.

By this time the manager was out of his office saying what the chuffing hell is going on in my casino and the Chinese had rediscovered their tongues and were squawking like budgies on speed. And Titus was just standing there.

So the manager came over to him and said –You! Office.– And he marched off with Titus in tow.

A minute later the pit boss was called into the office. He was followed by the croupier, who was followed by two men from the Chinese group. We could hear them all shouting at each other and then suddenly it went dead quiet.

The next thing that happened was that the Chinese men came out looking as if they'd been kicked in the balls, which they probably had. Then the pit boss emerged followed by the croupier.

Then finally the manager came out, his arm around Titus's shoulder, and marched him up to the bar and ordered up a bottle of shampoo and a slap up dinner for us all.

And after that no one ever bothered Titus again. He had his position behind Rose's Mum's chair and if the Chinese ever got too noisy or rowdy he just gave them a look and they quietened down.

So that was another thing we learned about Titus. That as well as knowing everything there was to know about the night sky, he was also the strongest, and most honest, man on the beach.

* * *

I liked Smithy's Mum from the start. She never gave an inch if she thought she was right.

One evening she came round with a bottle of whisky and we laughed when I said to her that when we were at school everyone thought that she and Smithy's Dad were high up Communist spies.

–Smithy's Dad caught a bullet in the leg fighting in Spain. That's all. Though as far as I was concerned, he was the most romantic man who ever walked the face of the earth.–

–What did he do after Spain?–

–A bit of this and a bit of that. Trades Unions. CP. Morning Star. The usual.–

–Bit of spying too?–

–You make him sound like a traitor. But who's the real patriot? Someone who just wants to make the world a better place or someone like Billy who rapes and steals his way through life?–

Before I could answer she went on. –We're on the same side Arthur. You and me and Smithy and his dad and the others. We do what we think is right.–

–Was I right to kill Billy then?–

–No, of course you weren't.–

She stopped. She could see I looked shocked. Then she said –You should have kidnapped him and threatened to cut off his knob if he didn't give all his money to the poor.–

We both laughed at that and had another glass of whisky.

* * *

And so life on the beach continued.

One day I was looking down on to the beach from the bench outside the chalet when I saw a man I was sure was the piggy-eyed doctor who had given me the wrong diagnosis in the first place.

I said to Rose –I'll be back in a moment. I've got some business to see to.–

I was angry. I ran quickly down the path, past Titus and Rose's Mum's chalet and then onto the beach and on towards my man. He had his back to me and was walking away.

If that nutjob had done his job properly I wouldn't be

a chuffing fugitive and facing the rest of my life behind bars if I was found.

I caught up with him, put my hand on his shoulder and turned him round and said –Remember me then doc?–

–You what?–

He was twenty years older and a plumber from Barnsley on holiday with his family.

–I gave him a scare anyway,– I said to Rose later. –That'll teach him to look like a doctor.–

But she wasn't amused. –You carry on like that Arthur you'll get us both caught.–

* * *

But most of the time we lived quietly enough.

We became friends with Leo the Artist who lived further along the cliff. He was painting experimentally. He was elongating his figures and his landscapes and at the same time pushing and changing colours as far as they would go.

His chalet was lined with canvasses. I could see how he'd pushed the colour in his seas to the darkest blue. His skies and clouds were red and yellow.

I told him how Titus had said I should try to paint the night sky and the stars. I wanted to tell him about the picture I'd painted of the Touareg in the desert when I was in jail, but I stopped myself.

There were times down there on the beach when it was easy to forget that I was a dangerous desperado on the run. It would have been easy to give myself away.

But Leo never asked too many questions. We stuck to talking about painting and cards and life on the beach, even though I'm sure he knew something was up.

* * *

I loved life on the beach with Rose and the others. The sea, the cliff, these things became our life. Walking barefoot through the shallows with Rose, or picking mussels and watching the gulls made me happy. It was difficult to believe that any other world had ever existed.

But then one day Frank turned up with our new passports. He also told us that the police and the Ratcatchers were planning a new drive to catch me and that it was time to move on.

–How did you swing these Frank?– I asked, turning the pages of the passports and looking at our pictures and our new identities.

He touched the side of his nose with his finger. –People with connections Arthur.–

I took a guess. –Do you mean people with connections like Ivan in Russia?–

–More than my life's worth, Arthur,– he replied.

* * *

We spent hours yakking about where we could go.

I said to Rose's Mum –Do you still want me to come out and run the *Bloods Head* bar in Thailand?–

She shook her head. –No thanks Arthur, not now. Giving up *Bloods Head* bar.–

–Still worried about the Cambodian hit man?–

–Yeah, life getting too dangerous there. He always looking for me.– She turned to Titus and gave his arm a squeeze. –Anyway I got my new man here.–

Yeah and his pension I thought.

But then neither of them seemed to be complaining too much. It seemed a case of two oddballs together. We went through all the places desperados are supposed to go, the Australian outback, the Greek Islands, the Costa del Sol.

In the end Rose said –Why don't we let the box decide.–

I looked at her. –Yeah and end up like Dozey Dave in Murmansk.–

–Well, he's happy enough isn't he?–

–Yeah,– I said. –He sounds like he is.–

He had sent a card to the *Albert Arms* a month ago saying he'd been made foreman of the fish processing plant and that his wife was expecting a baby.

* * *

In the end we decided to have a send off party.

I could see Frank looking worried. –The police are bound to find out, they're still watching everyone.–

I waved the passports in his face. –By the time they get themselves organised we'll be long gone. And with these they won't know who they're looking for either.–

Rose added –And with the box choosing the destination they won't know where to look.–

Then I said –Unless they bring the box in and threaten to break its arms if it doesn't tell them!– which got a laugh.

–I know we won't be here then, but I still don't like the idea of the police and the journalists going through all our stuff. It gives me the creeps,– Rose added thoughtfully.

–I know how you feel,– I said. –But you can't just go off without saying goodbye to your mates can you?–

* * *

We stood on the cliff top and watched Frank's white van coming towards us.

–It's like one of those old films,– I said to Rose. –When the workers all get on a charabanc to go to the seaside for their annual holidays.–

Ivan, dressed in his black security guard's uniform with the red snarling dog insignia on the shoulders, was sitting in the front passenger seat next to Frank.

He got out first.

–Everything present and correct Arthur. Safe journey down. No trouble. No tail.–

–Thanks Ivan.–

Next came Ivan's Wife, followed by Stan brushing off his suit and squinting into the sunlight, then Nell and Nancy and Albert and Albert's Wife and Benny and then even Hemlock, looking healthy and tanned, and finally Smithy who took a deep breath of sea air and said it was good to be home.

We were about to turn away when Ivan suddenly shouted –STOP!– and we all turned back.

–Party's not over yet.–

So we looked back to see Hong Kong Jimmy clambering out of the van, sweating and carrying a load of his Chinese cooking pots.

–Arsing van. Smell like the monkey's bum in there. Plods catch you Arthur, they going to whack your arse.–

Haw haw haw.

–Good to see you too Jimmy,– I said.

I could see Stan looking up the cliff road before turning and muttering something to Nell. Finally a taxi came round the corner and pulled up.

–Another little surprise in the bag for you Arthur,– Ivan said.

The elegant South American lady stepped out of the car and smiled and I knew who she was straight away.

I'd thought at the time you didn't take a package holiday from Venezuela just to show off the old family photos.

Stan said –I'd like to introduce my ex-wife Mercedes from Venezuela.–

–Arthur my dear.– Her lips touched my cheek and I smelt the rich perfume. –You are such a hero in my country.–

But my eyes were on the chubby young man in a suit, smoking a cigarette, who had got out of the taxi after her. He had a round face and wore glasses.

She turned to him. –And of course my son Manuel.–

–Who's come to see his long lost dad.–

–Precisely.–

Mumble, mumble, fag ash, fag ash, except in Spanish.

I looked at Stan. –What are you going to do then? Open up a branch office in Venezuela?–

–He's very good with figures, Arthur.–

Finally we rescued Smithy's dog, which had been sick in the back of the van, and went down to the chalet.

* * *

We threw caution to the winds. Even if the police and the Ratcatchers were on to us, by the time they got down here we would be gone.

Smithy produced the banners and flags his Mum had made for our campaign to save Athletic.

Any ship out in the bay would have seen a large white flag with red lettering stitched on to it which read

Those with Benefit Books shall be given Rolls Royces,

*And those with Rolls Royces shall be given Benefit
Books.*

And any Ratcatcher on the cliff top looking down
with his binoculars would have seen a flag draped
across the back of the chalet which read

*And the Journalists shall become Ratcatchers,
And the Ratcatchers shall become Journalists.*

Then on one end of the chalet we hung the flag
which had the cartoon figure of Billy pissing on an
outline of the continent of Africa.

Finally we persuaded Manuel to climb on to the roof
and lay the last flag there, BALLS TO BILLY, for any
passing plane to see.

After that Rose's Mum and Titus and Leo and
Smithy's Mum and a few others from the beach
joined us. Then Hong Kong Jimmy and Rose's Mum
cooked up a feast and we spent the afternoon
yakking outside.

We learned that Albert's Wife had changed her mind
about renaming the *Albert Arms* the *King Charles.*
She now wanted to call it the *King William.*

Then Mercedes touched me on the arm. She had
those dark South American eyes you see in films.

–In Venezuela we adore a man with cojones. They
would erect a statue to you there Arthur, not put you
in prison.–

We looked over at father and son deep in conversation.

–And he's such a clever child. Just like his father.–

Rose said Hemlock had fallen in love with a saleswoman called Betty from Belfast. –Guess what she
sells?–

I thought for a moment, imagining Betty arriving at

the door of the *Suk U Dry* Care and Rest Home with her saleswoman's briefcase. Then I said –How about dog biscuits?–

And Rose roared with laughter.

Finally Hemlock came up to me and shook my hand. I could see the scar on the side of his head.

–Congratulations Arthur,– he said. –You certainly beat the odds that time.–

I imagined him slumped over a table, blood pouring out of his head wound and a crowd of South American dock workers planning to throw his body into the harbour.

–Business still thriving then?–

–Too right. The inspectors say they've never seen a home like it.–

We both laughed.

–Been anywhere nice for your holidays this year?–

–Betty and I are buying a villa in Spain.–

–Safer than …–

–… Scotland.–

We both laughed again. The Chinese money had been right, Hemlock was certainly a case.

Frank called for silence and I stood up. –The last time we were all together I was in the dock and that evil case in a horse hair wig was banging me up for life.–

Laugh, laugh.

As I talked I could see Leo whispering urgently to Frank. I went on –But how times have changed. My illness has gone, prison has gone and Athletic is saved. Sometimes I think it's a dream and I'll wake up back in the nick with screws banging doors and shouting.–

Frank was looking up at me.

I went on quickly –So I give you all a toast. The future!–

They roared and clapped.

Then Frank said –Leo says there's a bloke on the cliff top looking down with a pair of binoculars.–

–Thanks Frank.–

I sent Titus and Ivan and Ivan's Wife up to investigate. When they returned they were carrying a mobile phone, a trilby hat with a feather in it, a notebook and a small bottle of whisky.

–You didn't give him a chance to use the phone?–

–No way boss,– said Ivan. –We whacked him from behind while he was having a pee.–

–Where is he now?–

The three of them cracked their knuckles in unison.

–Let's just say he ain't going to be doing any more writing in this parish for a while,– said Ivan.

Haw, haw, haw.

I opened the notebook and read the childish writing. "11.00 hours arrive Cornwall."

–Seems like we caught him in time,– I said. –But there are bound to be others. What was he like?–

Ivan held his nose –Bit whiffy boss.–

–Where have you put him?–

–In one of the empty chalets.–

When it was getting dark I went up with Ivan and Frank to look at him.

Frank opened the door and I peered inside.

There was an overpowering smell and I saw two red piggy eyes staring back at me out of the corner. Then there was a scuffling and he disappeared into the back of the chalet.

–Keep him here till we've gone,– I said to Ivan as we locked the door and went back down. –They're tricky bastards and we don't want any trouble.–

–Right oh boss.–

* * *

Later when it was dark and the moon was up and the stars were out Smithy's Mum put on some music. Titus and Rose's Mum began to dance, then Stan and Mercedes joined them and eventually Rose and I got up too and I could feel the music running through me.

I woke up with a start in the middle of the night. There was the sound of the sea on the shore below and I could hear Nell and Smithy talking quietly. Then I heard the noise again, a faint scratching from the back window.

Getting up I tiptoed over. When I opened the shutter I heard the scurrying sound of a light-footed Rat-catcher running off into the bushes.

Half an hour later with the sun starting to come up I woke Rose and we got dressed.

–There's no more time,– I said. –They'll bring in reinforcements and then the police will be here.–

Outside, as the morning began to spread out over the bay, we placed the magic box on the table in front of us. I opened it and Rose took out the dice.

–I wonder where we'll get?– I said.

–I don't mind as long as we're together,– she replied.

So we threw the dice and made our way up to the cliff top where Titus was ready with the car.

We rolled the dice and arrived in Morocco, via Blackpool and Murmansk.

In Blackpool we stayed in a guest house run by a miserable thin beef who said if he had his time again he'd emigrate to China.

–That's the future mate,– he said, as he served us breakfast. –The Land of The Rising Sun and Chairman Mao. You buy a dishwasher from that lot you know it's going to work. Not like the rubbish you get here.–

After that we rolled the dice again and arrived in Murmansk. I could see the Russian cabbie checking us out in the rear view mirror.

–Where you from?– he said after a bit.

–England.–

He started to laugh and passed back a copy of the morning paper. –That your lot then?–

I could see him grinning at me in the mirror.

We looked down at a picture of a starving Chinese man dropping a dog into a cooking pot.

I passed the paper back. –Nice try, wrong country.–

I looked out of the window at the dreary apartment buildings and factories covered in snow and ice.

It was my turn now. –I had a mate who came here once. He said it was great. He said you could shag any bird you wanted for a bag of nuts.–

After that he put his foot down and when we came to the hotel he snarled at me in Russian when I didn't give him a tip.

We ate dinner in a restaurant where the waiter wore cardboard shoes and the only thing on the menu was cabbage soup.

I thought of Smithy's Mum and wondered what she'd seen in the place.

The next day we went out to the factory where

Dozey Dave worked, but it was all closed up. The man on the gate was wearing a big fur hat. He told us –It's a holiday mate. They've all gone to the beach.–

–Oh yeah?–

Then he went back inside his cabin and we had a nose around for a bit. Everything creaked and groaned in the wind.

Rose shivered. –This place gives me the creeps,– she said.

–Me too.–

After that we rolled the dice again and the next plane took us to Morocco.

Mohammed, grinning from ear to ear, met us at the airport.

–Where you been Brother. Everybody's been waiting for you.–

–Sorry about that Mo. After you busted me out of prison we got delayed a bit.–

–In Cornwall.–

–And Blackpool.–

–And Murmansk. -

* * *

We soon settled into our new life in Casablanca, finding an apartment with a roof terrace that over-looked the bay. In the morning we ate our breakfast on the terrace with the scent of oranges and jasmine wafting up from the street below. And in the evening we sipped a glass of wine as the sun set over the bay and Rose would say –If you ask me Blair got it wrong. There is nothing really wrong with the Arabs at all.–

And I would reply –Yes, I think he's definitely bombing the wrong country.–

–He should be bombing Murmansk.–
–Or Blackpool.–
Which made us both laugh.

* * *

Mo was in business with his brother, the case who had been driving the getaway car when I had been busted out of prison. They were making jeans on two floors of a disused warehouse in Casablanca.

When the jeans were finished they were taken by truck to a desert camp. There they were loaded on to camels, supervised by Omar the Camel Man, and smuggled across the border into Algeria where they were traded for more camels which were then brought back and sold in Morocco.

One day after work Mo told me that he planned to make the business legitimate in future and that he wanted me to be director of exports for Europe.

But when I mentioned this to his brother in his office the following day he just giggled and looked the other way.

* * *

One day I saw our pictures on the front page of *Le Matin*, the local paper.

I yelled up to Rose –Pack your bags. Bring the box. The nutballs are on to us again.–

But when Mohammed translated the article he almost wet himself laughing.

–Hey, Bro, you in real big trouble now. Sounds like you going to get cuffed up again.–

Finally he read out what the government Ratcatchers had written.

–"Rejoice! The Kingdom of Morocco is safe!

–"Rejoice! The assassin Polianski and his sidekick Rose are with us no more!

–"Rejoice! The fantastic duo have returned to England after the collapse of their crooked timeshare company in Portugal!"–

–That's Frank's work,– I said.

Mohammed had met Frank when he had come to see me in prison. I said –Frank could sell the papers anything. He could tell them that the General's knob was two foot long and drank Milk Stout and they'd shout HOLD THE FRONT PAGE and bring out a special edition.–

* * *

Most evenings we went to Saleem's café overlooking the bay to drink mint tea and eat ice cream. Apart from Rose and me there was Eric the German, who was Mohammed's fixer, Eric's girlfriend Hannah, Mohammed's brother and Omar the Camel Man who never said anything.

We would watch the football on TV and yak about what had happened during the day, and Rose would read out the letters that Nancy had written from home.

One day we heard that Athletic had been promoted back up from the Conference to the League, which cheered me up.

The next day we heard that Stan the Owl was planning to open up a branch office of the betting shop in Venezuela.

And the day after that Hemlock and Belfast Betty were planning to get married.

Then one evening, when there was no football on the TV, I brought the box in to Saleem's.

I passed it round so everyone could see it. Then I

told them that Frank and Nancy had bought it in a town in the south of Morocco when they had come here for a motorbike rally.

After that I told them that we had used it to invent Sure Start holidays and that it had sent Dozey Dave to Murmansk and ordered a lot of daft things in Hong Kong Jimmy's Chinese restaurant before eventually bringing Rose and me here to Morocco.

Everyone held it and weighed it in their hands and opened it up and looked at the dice inside. Then they all said they had never seen anything like it in their lives before.

But there was a very strange occurrence. When it came to Omar the Camel Man's turn, he looked at the box suspiciously and sniffed at it. Then he put it quickly back down on the table, whispered something in Mohammed's ear and got up and walked out, just like that.

–What's up Mo?– I said. –Is Omar allergic to boxes or what?–

–No Arthur,– Mo replied. –He just said the box doesn't smell like any camel bone box he ever smelt before.–

Then he looked at me and added –He also said you are meddling in things you don't understand.–

Which brought the conversation to an end.

* * *

Eric the German was Mohammed's fixer who sorted everything out.

He had a crew cut and a gold tooth and wore dark glasses he never took off. He spoke English with a sloppy American accent.

Mohammed said –Eric's a tough guy Arthur. Done five years in the Spanish Foreign Legion. He speaks

Arabic and Berber and navigates through the desert by the stars.–

But Eric wasn't an easy case to talk to. Sometimes I'd ask him a question and I wouldn't get a reply at all, though I knew he was staring at me hard through his dark glasses.

* * *

Eric's girlfriend Hannah was the complete opposite. She was from Austria and she ran a co-op for women who had been abused or thrown out by their ever-loving Moroccan husbands.

Eric and Mohammed said the co-op was a waste of time but Rose and I were for it.

Rose said –You should see the way those poor women look at her. They think she's wonderful.–

I could see what they meant. How would you feel if you were thrown out on your arse with nothing and a strange Austrian woman set up a co-op which gave everyone a chance?

One evening Rose said to her –Why don't you tell Arthur the story of how you ended up here?–

–No,– she replied. –I am sure Arthur would much rather be watching the football with Eric and Mohammed.–

–No,– Rose said. –Arthur wants to hear your story.–

So she took a sip of her mint tea and began. –For twenty five years I was a model employee of the *Blue Danube* insurance company of Vienna, Austria.

–I was never late and I kept errors to a minimum. I always smiled and I was always polite to the customers, even the most difficult ones.

–But at the same time I had also eaten enough cream cake and wiener schnitzel to sink the entire Austrian navy twice over.–

I looked at her. It was difficult to see the Hannah sitting in front of us now, trim and confident, eating cream cakes and wiener schnitzel in an Austrian insurance office.

She continued –Then one day I was with my mother feeding the ducks by the lakeside when I said to her "Living this way I am killing myself."

–So I went to the actuarial tables which we used to calculate the life span of our customers and I calculated that if I did not change I had only three years left to live.

–So I was wondering what I should do when the managing director of the *Blue Danube* insurance company, a tall man with dark hair, called me into his office and said, "Congratulations Hannah, you are a model employee. You have done more than your duty. You have eaten enough cream cakes and wiener schnitzel to sink the entire Austrian navy twice over. As a reward we have decided to give you a year off before you die."

–Of course all my colleagues said, "She will go to a Greek island and lie in the sun and have a torrid affair with the restaurant waiter," but I didn't.–

–So what did you do Hannah?– I asked.

–I watched a programme on the television about people who had changed their lives by walking the old Pilgrim route to Spain and I did that instead.–

–How long did it take you Hannah?– Rose asked.

–Eight months.–

–And how far was it?–

–Three thousand miles.–

–And how many pairs of shoes did you wear out?–

–Four.–

–And what did you see?–

–I saw mountains and forests and rivers and beautiful churches.–

–And how much weight did you lose?–

–Twenty five kilos.–

–And what did you do when you saw a bear in the woods?–

–I ran for my life!–

We all laughed at that.

–And when you arrived at Santiago Compostela?–

–I walked in to the cathedral and stood before the box which, according to the legend, contains the bones of St James.–

–What!– I shouted. –Not another chuffing box!– And we all laughed again.

But then I asked –So what happened next?–

–I sent an email to the *Blue Danube* insurance company thanking them for the year off but saying that my life had changed completely and that it was no longer my intention to return.–

–And what did they say?–

–They replied saying that I was no longer a model employee and they intended to bankrupt me and take all my money to protect the interests of the shareholders.–

We both looked at her, shocked.

–An hour later I was sitting on the bench outside the cathedral thinking about what I was going to do when I saw Eric for the first time. He had been walking the same Pilgrim route.

–I told him that my employer, the *Blue Danube* insurance company of Vienna, planned to bankrupt me to protect the interests of their shareholders.–

–And what did he propose?–

–He said he was planning to return to Morocco and that I could come with him if I wanted. And so I did.–

–And what did the insurance company do?–

–Some months later the managing director sent me a personal letter congratulating me on my decision and saying that he planned to follow in my footsteps shortly.–

–And did he?–

–Not yet. He still has to wait until he is released from prison for defrauding the pension fund!–

We all roared with laughter.

* * *

Hannah sold her house in Austria and used the money to open the small co-operative in Casablanca.

She has a dozen women, who would otherwise be out begging or whoring or having the shit beaten out of them, working at sewing machines, making sweaters and blouses and what-nots and keeping the profits for themselves.

Other women sort out the cash and the sales. It is all run on a co-operative basis with everything divided up equally. They have even started literacy classes for the women and their children. Two afternoons a week Rose goes in to help.

Hannah said the women who worked in the co-op were better off than the people Mohammed and his brother employed in the factory making jeans.

She told Mohammed –You are exploiting the people who work for you. They are poor people and illegal migrants from Niger and Mali. They have nothing.–

But Mohammed replied that he was giving them work and money and if it wasn't for him they would be out in the street with nothing at all, and if they didn't like it they were free to try their hand elsewhere.

* * *

When we heard the stories Hannah told us about what the women had to put up with from their men-

147

folk I said to Rose –They must have a special class in school here. Men only. It's called How to Scramble Your Wife's Brains, Fuck Up Your Children's Futures And Generally Act Like A Complete Arsehole. It's the only class some of them ever attend. The rest of the time they're out playing football.–

Specifically there's the dodge where the husband abandons the wife and kids but stops her going ahead with a divorce by not turning up to hearings, leaving her with NOTHING. You even have to buy your own begging bowl round here.

–Why doesn't he let her go through with the divorce so she can get on with her life?– Rose asked.

–Because he's a big-arsed Moroccan who wants to show he's chief boss in his own toilet,– I replied.

Sometimes I wanted to go into a café where all the men were sitting around on their fat backsides and shout –Get up off your fat Moroccan backsides and sort yourselves out and get this place tidied up. And stop abusing your women and everyone else or I am going to come back and hose you out.–

But of course I didn't, because I didn't want to have my throat cut and also because I admired the way they dealt with everything else they had to put up with and still retained their dignity and manners.

Mohammed laughed at Hannah and Eric said she was full of "dopey talk." But I knew she was right.

So I don't care that Eric sneered or that Mohammed looked down his nose.

Because in my book Hannah had got it dead right. SHE HAD CHANGED HER LIFE AND CHANGED THE LIFE OF OTHERS AROUND HER.

And if only a hundred other women (or a thousand, or ten thousand) from Britain or Germany or Austria or Canada followed her example, we would start to get somewhere.

* * *

After three months this is my assessment of life in Morocco.

Things I hate about Morocco:
1. Fat nutballs (Moroccan) who refuse to give up their seats on buses to pregnant women with children.
2. Kings (Moroccan) who don't shave so that they look like Mexican gangsters.
3. Businessmen (Moroccan) who drive Mercedes while women who could be their mothers live worse than dogs in the *bidonvilles.*
4. Government Ratcatchers (Moroccan) who state, in articles in *Le Matin,* that poverty will decrease by fifteen per cent a year for the next ten years.
5. Householders (Moroccan) who are too lazy to fix the drains or clean the toilets or paint the fronts of their houses.
6. Tourists (French) who earn a hundred thousand a year, but who are too mean to give a penny to a beggar.

Things that I like about Morocco:
1. Women (Moroccan) who make the sound a cooing dove makes when they call out their husbands' names.
2. Bus drivers (Moroccan) who are prepared to carry a live sheep in the hold of their bus as if it were a suitcase or a bicycle.
3. Heads of Households (Moroccan) who put a pilgrimage to Mecca before a new car.
4. Students (Moroccan) who choose mint tea rather than cheap lager on a night out.
5. Taxi drivers (Moroccan) who squeeze seven passengers into an old Mercedes.

6. People (Moroccan) who have got manners and dignity. No one here has told me to arse off. The people here are human beings who live in a harsh land where the light is bright and shadowless.

Final thing that I HATE:
Tourists who gorge and stare as if they are on a visit to the zoo.
–Throw a penny to the seal Marjorie, see if he'll whistle out of his bum.–
I see the tourists as dead pieces of meat being carted around on charabancs.
–Stare at the clown. That'll be sixpence.–
Or –Oh, look at that beggar, he's got no arms.–

And there is something else that should be asked of forward thinking Moroccans. And that is: What have you done with the other half of the population, namely the women?
Either you release them voluntarily or we will be forced once again to let loose that Dog of War, General (Sir Anthony) Blair, to bring them blinking into the sunlight from whatever cave you have hidden them in, battered and bruised and wrapped in table cloths. And once again the General will be our hero and raise his arms aloft to the world!

* * *

One morning I was sitting in Saleem's café reading *Le Matin* and looking out to sea. Rose and Hannah were sitting at the next table yakking and eating ice cream.
I had said to Rose the night before –You want to watch it Rose. You keep on eating ice cream like that you are going to blow up as fat as a balloon.–

But Rose didn't care. She was happy here.

She opened a letter from Nancy and called out –Listen to this Arthur.–

There was always news from home.

Yesterday it was –Smithy's broken his leg in Timbuctoo and his mum is going to fetch him home in the air ambulance.–

The day before it had been –Nell's going out with Manuel to open the branch office in Venezuela, and Albert's Wife is going to call the pub the *King Harry*.–

And today –Hemlock's getting married to Belfast Betty in Iceland.–

–Iceland?– I looked out over the bay. –What the chuffing hell is Hemlock doing getting married in Iceland?–

Rose read the letter again. –No, it's Nancy's writing. They're getting married in Ireland.–

–Right,– I said and took a sip of my mint tea. –That's more like it.–

Just then Eric came in and sat down and ordered a mint tea from Saleem.

Saleem was a thin beef who never smiled and who was best friends with Omar the Camel Man. He had a wife who he kept wrapped up in a bed sheet in the back, and who no one had ever seen. His only pleasure in life was watching the football on the TV in the café. It didn't matter where it was from. One time I found him watching the Latvian Cup Final at midnight.

Eric took a sip of his mint tea and then said in his drippy American voice –We're going over the border next week, if you want to join us Arthur.–

I was about to reply –No thanks, Eric, I've never been on a camel in my life,– when Rose butted in and said

–Arthur can't go over the border, Eric. He's never been on a camel in his life.–

Which clinched it. I turned to Eric and said –Yeah! Why not, Eric, it'll be a pleasure.–

He turned and grinned at me behind his sunglasses.

That evening I had to tell Rose to calm down. She didn't like Eric.

–He comes home with lipstick on his collar and has Hannah in tears.–

I wanted to say that Eric and his knob were well known in every back alleyway in Casablanca and that if the only thing he ever came back with was lipstick on his collar, Hannah should get down on her knees and give thanks. But I didn't.

Instead I said –Don't worry, Mohammed and Omar will be in charge.–

Since the occurrence with the box, Omar the Camel Man had been avoiding me, so the next day it was Saleem who came round to the factory in the lunch hour with an old camel and led me round on a rein so I could get the hang of it.

And that was my training for our great adventure in the desert.

* * *

Mohammed said we needed a swirling desert storm to hide us from the Algerian Border Guard when we crossed the border. As we waited for the right night, Eric told us stories of his life in the Spanish Foreign Legion.

Every day at the factory or at Saleem's if there was no football on it would be –We had to force march all day through the desert on half a cup of water.–

Or –When you're in a fire fight you always save the last bullet for yourself.–

And even one day –I fired a native out of the barrel of a canon when he refused to tell us where the enemy were.–

Until we were all so fed up with listening to him that I said –Well go on then Eric, how many people have you shot then really.–

He turned and grinned until I could see the sun glistening on his gold tooth. He raised his left hand and extended five fingers and then raised his right and extended a further five fingers, making ten in all.

Then he turned to me and said –Well, beat that partner.–

But I could remember Billy's brains dripping down on top of me and the stink of his piss and vomit, so I just got up and walked out and left him alone.

But the incident made me think. And that night I said to Rose as we were sitting on our roof terrace sipping wine and looking out over the bay –I don't think Eric ever was in the Spanish Foreign Legion.–

Rose looked surprised. –What makes you say that Arthur?–

I thought for a moment and said –Spanish Legionnaires are supposed to be silent and mysterious. They're not meant to say if they've fired a native out of the barrel of a canon.–

Rose nodded. –I was wondering about that.–

–About what?–

–About what it's like to be fired out of the barrel of a canon.–

We both looked out over the bay as we pondered that one.

Finally I said –He's probably just a German bus driver who got fed up with taking his holidays in Benidorm and decided to take on a new persona. He's probably got a wife and children back home in Germany wondering where he is.–

Rose giggled at that and said –Don't tell Hannah, she'll be ever so disappointed.–

* * *

We arrived at the desert camp just as the sun was setting.

I got out of the jeep and looked at the brown tents set against the dunes and the men in black loading up the camels.

Mo touched my arm and pointed to a low ridge to the East. –The Algerian frontier.–

An hour later the night was clear and the stars were sparkling.

I turned to Mohammed. –We are lit up like the Blackpool Illuminations Mo.–

Mohammed grinned. –Don't worry about it Bro.–

After Saleem had cooked dinner and Eric and Omar had loaded up the camels, I looked up at the sparkling stars again.

I was about to shout out to Eric –You got the forecast wrong tonight you great big German bus driver,– when a first breath of wind touched my face and in a minute the sky darkened and the brilliant sparkling stars disappeared.

Then Eric clapped his hands and shouted out –OK men let's go.–

And so we filed out into the swirling desert storm, our faces covered with thick scarves against the biting sand.

We were Eric in the lead followed by Omar, followed by Mohammed, followed by Saleem and myself, followed by the other camel men.

We would stop if Eric heard a noise above the storm or if he spotted a light. Then he would give a signal and we would change direction and continue.

The soft sand turned to hard pebbles and we drew our scarves tighter round our faces. I thought of Rose in our apartment overlooking the bay in Casablanca.

Last night she had been in tears. –You are bound to be captured Arthur,– she had said. –You had better write your will.–

So I crossed my fingers, remembering that the last time, after I had gone to prison, she had spent all our money, and wrote, "I leave everything I own to Bangkok Rose. Signed Arthur Polianski." I put it on the table in the morning when I left, while Rose was still in bed asleep.

Eric came down the line and put his finger to his lips and whispered that we were passing the Algerian Border Guard fort.

Then we stopped again and Mohammed came down the line and said –We there now Arthur. We waiting for the other guys to show.–

And soon they did, emerging like ghosts out of the storm to unload our panniers.

I imagined the Algerian Border Guards in their border fort peering out into the night searching for us.

Then the ghostly figures disappeared back into the night and we turned for home. Because the panniers were now empty we rode up on the camels. My eyes started to close and my head slumped forward till it touched Saleem's neck.

Using the system Gerald the Irish Screw had taught me in prison I replayed my last visit to the factory where the jeans were made.

It was early afternoon and I was on my way to see Mohammed. I was walking along the corridor feeling the warm concrete under my feet.

I passed the door of an office that was half open and saw Mohammed's brother, wreathed in hashish smoke, sitting at the desk speaking on the phone. I took a pace forward, but then I stopped and stepped back and looked down.

A shaft of light from the open window had illuminated a box at the side of the desk that I had missed the first time I walked past.

Inside the box were piled up a mass of opaque plastic bags filled with creamy chalk-like powder.

I stopped, stunned.

My gaze went up again to Mohammed's brother, wreathed in hashish smoke, and then down again to the box filled with opaque plastic bags of the creamy chalk-like powder.

In Morocco there is only one type of creamy chalk-like substance that is packed in opaque plastic bags and that is drugs, i.e. cocaine or heroin.

I opened my eyes, sat bolt upright on the camel and shouted out into the swirling desert storm –JEANS FACTORY MY CHUFFING ARSE!–

Which was exactly when Eric also shouted out –IT'S THE BORDER GUARD!–

I turned to see the headlights of a dozen jeeps coming at us through the wind and the storm.

WE HAD BEEN RUMBLED!

Suddenly Saleem kicked his heels into the side of the camel and we shot forward.

Suddenly there was no time to think about Mohammed and drugs.

Suddenly we were a band of desperados fleeing for our lives into the night!

Eric yelled out directions and we dodged first to the left and then to the right, trying to throw off our pursuers.

I turned to look again. The headlights were sharper. The border guard's jeeps were gaining!

The next thing that happened was that a burst of tracer fizzed over our heads into the night.

FIZZ FIZZ, CRACK CRACK.

Then Eric yelled again and Saleem and the other camel men pulled hard on their reins and we shuddered to a halt in the lee of a dune and leaned forward to make ourselves as small as we could in the cold and the swirling sand.

Counting. Twenty seconds, thirty, forty …

Until with a fizz of tracer and a wail of sirens the jeeps of the Algerian Border Guard raced past us and on into the storm.

After that we waited for an hour before leaving the protection of the dune and inching our way home, changing direction if we saw a light and stopping to listen if we heard the sound of an engine, until finally as dawn broke and the storm abated we limped into camp and got off our camels and slumped to the ground exhausted.

So that was how we discovered that Eric was in fact a proper desert guide and without doubt a real true life Spanish Foreign Legionnaire.

And that was also how I discovered that Mohammed and his brother were smuggling things other than jeans across the Algerian border.

Which, as we made our way back out of the desert and over the mountains and back to Casablanca, led me to formulate a plan.

* * *

This was how I put my plan into action. It was a week later and I was in Saleem's café with Mohammed. Saleem was in the far corner watching the Mongolian Cup Final on the TV.

I took a deep breath and said –I know what you are up to Mo.–

He turned to me –How do you mean Arthur?–

He looked nervous.

–It's what I saw Mo.–

–What did you see Arthur?–

–Little white packets in the office Mo.–

Mo looked worried.

–You not supposed to put your nose in the office Arthur. You keep on putting your nose in the office one day you going to get it bitten off.–

Then he leaned forward and said –I busted you out of jail Arthur. You owe me.–

But I wasn't afraid of Mo. So I squared up to him and said –And I'm the guy who whacked Billy.–

–Yeah well.– Mo had no answer to that.

So I picked up my mint tea and went over to join Saleem watching the Mongolian Cup Final and left Mo to stew for a bit.

In the end I judged it just right. Because when the game was over and I picked up the paper and walked back to the table, Mo was sitting looking at me, biting his nails.

So I said casually –If you ask me it's disgusting Mo.–

–What is Arthur?–

–What goes on outside.–

He looked out into the street.

–The people who haven't got anything. Left to rot like so much meat gone off.–

He turned to me angrily. –What do you expect me to do about it Arthur? I'm a businessman. I can't go handing out cash to everyone.–

So under my breath I said –We'll see about that.–

And went out into the street and told a woman who was sitting cross legged on the ground under a bed sheet with her hand out begging for pennies to come inside.

When she was sitting at the table with a glass of mint tea in front of her, I lifted the edge of the bed sheet to expose a shrivelled up little baby that was so feeble it couldn't even be bothered to cry out.

Then I said to Mo –Not to put too fine a point on it Mo, old boy, this little bundle of shit and bones which you pass twice a day, to and fro, on your way to the factory and back, and which could be your sister or brother, is actually at this moment in time starving to death.–

Mo looked shocked.

I upped the anger level. –This woman and her baby aren't extras in Lawrence of Arabia, Mo. They don't catch a bus home in the evening to a nice cosy pad or even a nice cosy jail cell. She lives on the street with nothing. THIS IS IT. This is real fucking life.–

Mo gawped at me, astonished, then recovered and leaned across the table and shouted in my face –YOU TELLING ME ARTHUR! THIS IS MY FUCKING COUNTRY! I KNOW WHAT GOES ON HERE!–

So now I shouted back –SURE YOU DO, AND YOU DO SOD ALL ABOUT IT LIKE EVERYONE ELSE HERE.–

Which shut him up. Finally he said –What do you want Arthur?–

So I turned to him, took a deep breath and gave him my list of demands.

* * *

So that is how a week later the workmen arrived at the door of Hannah's co-op.

The first thing they did was to trail an electric line from the factory to the co-op so that the women could have light and heat, especially in the winter when it is cold enough to freeze to death at night.

This was followed by a pipe for water so that the children and babies could be washed and mint tea prepared.

Following that an extension was built with bricks marked, in Arabic, "Property of Casablanca Council" and "Not To Be Removed", so that the children had a school room and women on the run from their ever-loving Moroccan husbands had a place to hide.

After that schoolbooks and pencils and chairs and desks also arrived, so that the children could learn to read and write properly.

And when it was all done we threw a party for the opening.

Rose and Hannah and all the women and children were there and we had ice cream and mint tea.

There was even a place for the woman from the street with the shrivelled up baby, which was already beginning to fatten out under the care of the other women.

Then Mohammed, dressed in his best suit, arrived with a Ratcatcher from *Le Matin* who stated in an article the following day that the generosity of citizens like Mohammed should make all Moroccans proud.

So that was how good relations, which had been strained between Mohammed and myself, were restored.

* * *

The next thing that happened was that we saw Leo in the main square in Marrakesh. We had finished early for the week in Casablanca and had taken the train up to Marrakesh to see the sights.

We were sitting in a café overlooking the main square when Rose said –Chuffing hell. That's Leo over there.–

–Where?–

–Over there.–

I followed the direction of her arm and saw him, tall and thin and looking in our direction.

–Jesus.–

I turned to Rose. –I hope he hasn't done a deal with the nutballs to betray us.– I stood up and shouted –Leo, over here mate. Chuffing hell.–

He looked round, finally picked us out, waved and came over.

After we'd shaken hands and he'd sat down and Rose had ordered mint tea I said –If you've come over here with Scotland Yard tucked up your backside you can think again Leo.–

I pointed to Mohammed and Eric. –All I've got to do is snap my fingers and these two dogs will cut your nuts off.–

I raised my hand.

–Arthur!– said Rose.

–You can go back to England if you want Rose, but nobody's cuffing me up again.–

I could see Leo looking worried. –No, I'm not with the law,– he said finally, –I'm on your side.–

–What about the *Tombola* reward?–

–I'm not after that either.–

–So how did you find us then? Did we leave a sign saying "Morocco bound" on the bedroom wall?–

–No. It wasn't me that found you. It was that camel bone box!–

Silence.

Then Rose said –That chuffing box. I'll strangle it one day.–

–When you went Frank told me the story of what the box could do. I drew a picture. Look.–

He pulled a square of drawing paper out of his shoulder bag and opened it up on the table.

He'd drawn a perfect replica of the box without ever seeing the chuffing thing!

–I began to dream about the box. It wouldn't leave me alone. In the end I went to the travel agent and told him to book me a ticket here. I had to see where Frank bought it.–

I looked at Rose. –That's what you said to me yesterday, that we have to find where the box came from.–

After that we ate dinner in the hotel, the seven of us, Rose, me, Eric, Hannah, Mohammed, Leo and Omar the Camel Man.

Over dinner Leo gave us news of the beach.

–After you went, the police and the journalists dragged all your stuff out and piled it up. Then they took turns to stand on top and have their pictures taken.–

I turned to Eric and said –You can turn your sights on that lot Eric. They're nothing but scum.–

There was a silence, then Rose changed the subject.

–What about mum and Titus then?–

–They're like a couple of newly-weds. Inseparable.–

–I hope they're not!– Rose said.

–Not what?– I asked.

–A couple of newly-weds.–

–Why not?–

–I meant to tell you. Just before we left mum said she'd forgotten to get divorced from the last one.–

–Jesus.–

There was a silence as we thought that one over.

To lighten the mood I asked –What news of the General then. Is he preparing another attack?–

–No. Not yet. But he's seen most mornings wearing a peaked cap and riding a white charger through Hyde Park,– Leo replied.

We all roared with laughter at that.

* * *

The following morning Eric and Mohammed hired a car and we set off south to the town where Frank and Nancy had bought the camel bone box.

There were seven of us, Rose, me, Mohammed, Eric and Hannah, Leo and Omar the Camel Man, who was driving. Eric and Mohammed sat in the front while the rest of us were in the back.

As we passed Touareg tribesmen in blue turbans riding on camels I told the story of the painting I had done for Whingeing Howard in prison and how it had ended up in *Tombola,* which gave them all a laugh.

Then Mohammed told them how he'd whistled up the guard dog in the prison and how it had taken a chunk out of the One Eyed Scotch Bastard's backside.

After that Eric told us about his first day in the Spanish Foreign Legion. –They buried us up to our necks in the sand and left us to fry in the midday sun.–

That stopped the conversation for a while. We all stared out at the passing desert.

Then Rose asked –Did they let you keep your sunglasses on Eric?– which brought us all out in fits of the giggles.

* * *

We stopped for lunch in a small town where a group of French tourists had got down from a coach and were nosing about in the market stalls.

Eventually they got settled in a restaurant, but when an old crone with no teeth stuck her palm out looking for money they had to stop talking and look down at their shoes and shuffle around and pretend she didn't exist.

So I got up, took a note out of my wallet, and walked

over and gave it to the old crone right in front of the tourists.

When I sat down again I could see Rose was embarrassed. –It's not just the French Arthur.–

–I know it's not Rose.–

I turned to look back at the tourists again. –It's the Germans, the Japanese, the whole lot of them. It's sickening. They come here on holiday gorging themselves when a crone like that hasn't got a bean.–

–What do you want them to do?– Rose asked.

I pointed to Hannah. –Follow her example.–

–What's that?–

–CHANGE YOUR LIFE.–

I numbered the points off on my fingers.

–Stop gorging on cream cakes.

–Walk a thousand miles on a rickety road.

–Stand in front of a magic box and repeat "I AM NOT GOING BACK TO BE TORTURED IN AN OFFICE WHERE THE BOSS HAS GOT PORK SCRATCHINGS FOR BRAINS AND WHERE MY LIFE IS DRIBBLING DOWN THE TOILET PAN."– I was in full flow. I had a lot more to say but Rose cut me short. She was angry now.

–You're a chuffing case Arthur. The tourists bring money. What do you want them to do, stop coming and stay at home?–

–Yeah. Good idea. Stay at home. Build another Peugeot. Have another squabble. Send the money instead. Good idea. Well done Rose.–

–They're not starving here Arthur,– Eric butted in.

–Oh yeah?– I stared at him. –Ask the crone I just gave the note to. Ask her when she last had a square meal. Ask her where she sleeps at night. Ask her how it feels to be turned down for a penny by a crowd of fat French tourists who've come to watch the freak show.–

That shut them all up.

* * *

After lunch, as we drove further south through the desert, we started to talk about the box.

Hannah said –I am an actuary, so I am for progress and science. I am not for fairies and hob-goblins and magic boxes.–

To which I replied –I am not a nutjob either but I will bet you that in a million years time all the White Coats will recognise that my little box has more of the answers than Einstein or Hawking.–

Rose giggled, but Hannah stared out of the window. Then she turned to me and said –That is really a very stupid point of view Arthur. You have obviously got something against science. Please do tell us what it is.–

–No, I've got nothing against science Hannah,– I replied. –I just want it to know its place, that's all. Let the box have a go every so often. Give the rest of us a chance to breathe.–

Eric heard this and turned round from the front. He'd been waiting to attack me.

–Next mosque please, driver,– he said in his sloppy American drawl. –Arthur needs to say his prayers.– Then he smiled at me. –Only kidding buddy. I'm with you really,– and he grinned and gave me his coded ten finger salute.

After that there was an awkward silence until Rose picked up Hannah's argument again.

–So how are you going to invent a cure for cancer or AIDS or get rid of the poverty you're always banging on about if you throw science out of the window and follow your little magic box?–

I had the answer there. –Look,– I said, leaning forward.

Rose, Hannah and Leo were all listening now. Even

Eric and Mohammed had turned down the radio in the front so they could hear.

–When Stephen Hawking finds a cure for AIDS I'll put up a statue to him in Trafalgar Square myself.

–But the point is that at the moment he and the other White Coats DON'T KNOW EVERYTHING. AND THEY MAY NOT EVEN BE ON THE RIGHT TRACK.–

At this Rose cut in. –Well I'd rather let Einstein or Hawking sort it out than have some chuffing box send you where you don't want to go and order daft stuff in restaurants.–

–Jesus Christ, Rose,– I shouted. I was angry now. –That's the chuffing point. The box broke every rule in the scientific book and there is no way that gob-shites like Hawking or Einstein can explain how.–

Rose had no answer to that, so I went on –And take Hannah as another example.–

Hannah glowered at me, but I was not going to be put off.

–She tells us she follows scientific principles but that's not true either. Look at what she did. Out of the blue she upped and walked three thousand miles along a rickety old road, following a path to a pile of old bones that almost certainly don't exist. And bang! her whole life changed and here she is in Morocco, and for the first time in her chuffing life she's doing something that MATTERS. Now where's the science in that?–

–But if it wasn't for science she wouldn't have the boots or the compass or the rest of the stuff that helped her to get there,– Rose replied.

–And if it wasn't for a pile of old bones in a box she would never have started out in the first place.–

After that we sat in silence for a bit. But half an hour later Hannah got her own back by asking me –Do you regret what you did Arthur?–

There was a silence and they all looked at me.

I know they wanted me to say yes, that I now saw that shooting Billy was the worst possible thing I could have done and that it would burden me forever.

But after a moment's pause I said –Not a bit of it. That little fucker tried to wreck my football club.–

* * *

The light was starting to fade when Eric pulled in to the side of the road and we pitched camp for the night.

Mohammed cooked dinner over a gas stove and we were relaxing and chatting under the stars when Hannah startled us by saying –The night that is rolling over us now will leave thousands dead by morning.– Which stopped us all dead in our tracks.

Then she explained to us that in this glorious scientific world of ours, this world of abundance, where there is enough for everyone, fifteen thousand children starve to death every day.

FIFTEEN THOUSAND CHILDREN
STARVE DAILY

Or

STARVING KIDDIE HORROR

Or *(Tombola)*

EARLY TO BED FOR AFRICAN TOTS

And in case you are wondering, death by starvation for a five year old is a slow and excruciatingly painful process. It's also extremely upsetting for those watching.

Textbook exercise (1): Write an essay describing your feelings as you watch your own children starve to death.

Textbook exercise (2): You are a television producer. Create original ways to visualise fifteen thousand dead children.

Hint: You could lay them head to toe so they stretched from Southampton to Aberdeen.
Hint: You could stand them on each other's shoulders so they made ten times the height of Buckingham Palace.

–Why?– said Leo.
–Why what?– asked Hannah.
–Why do we let them die?–
–Because they're black.–
–And African.–
–Or Asian.–
–Or South American.–
–Because they're small.–
–Because they're poor.–
–Because they're a long way from home.–
–Because they don't speak English.–
–Because they don't go to church.–
–Because deep in our hearts we don't believe they're the full human.–

Textbook exercise (3): Write an essay describing children starving to death on the streets of Birken-head or Swansea.

When Hannah had finished Eric and I got up and took the dishes and plates over to the car, where there was a water tank, and began to wash them. I could see Eric was unimpressed.

–Spend your life with dopey talk like that,– he grumbled, half to himself.

That got me going, so I said –You can't solve every problem by spraying bullets at it.–

He looked at me and laughed and replied –Oh yeah, well you didn't do too bad, did you?–

* * *

That night in the tent I had the strangest dream. I dreamt I was in a cabinet meeting with Blair. He was sitting on his horse at the head of the table and all the others were gathered round.

Someone said –If we give all the Iraqis Barclay Cards and tell them to go shopping that should solve the problem.–

At which Blair gave a laugh, but I wasn't sure whether it was him laughing or his horse.

I woke up and went outside and sat in the dark and looked up at the stars and thought about what Hannah had said, that fifteen thousand children starve to death every day.

I thought WHY DO PEOPLE PUT UP WITH IT ALL? If someone pushes them into the gutter, why don't they say –Arse off mate, mind where you're walking!–

What is it specifically that stops them?

Is it the certain knowledge that the police here administer electric shocks to those who step out of line? Or is it the certain knowledge that people who don't do as they're told in Morocco end up being put in coffin tombs for twenty years without being allowed to cut their hair or nails and have to live on cockroaches and every so often are taken out to have their genitals mutilated. And this information is then given to the journalists of *Le Matin* so that everyone knows to watch themselves?

Or can we blame the Men from the Mosques? And before anyone thinks of blowing me up I include here the Pope, the Archbishop of Canterbury, the Chief Druid and The Great White Rabbit.

Because I think that anyone who says that if you behave on this earth and don't cause trouble you will get virgins and waterfalls and flowers and blue skies and beer and port wine in the next world needs their arse kicking.

I would take them all, Kings, Queens, Bishops, Imams, Priests, Nuns, Monks, the whole lot, to some poor village in the mountains where it is still the MIDDLE AGES and I would show them the malnourished kids and I would say to the Chief Herbert –HOW DARE YOU ALLOW SOMETHING LIKE THIS.–

For Christ's sake the kids would go to school if you would just give them a sodding pencil to go with!

And its not just people here.

Why don't people everywhere say –No! Enough.–

Why don't the people of Glasgow (say) simply turn up at Balmoral (the Queen's Castle in Scotland, take the M8 out of Glasgow) and say –We demand recompense for wrongs done in years gone by. And while we are at it we want breakfast and room and board and we want it NOW.–

And if she threatens to call the police you say –We ARE the police!–

Have you any idea how rich the Queen is? Do you know that with a stroke of her pen she could organise Chinese dinners and horse races and villas in Spain for everyone and not feel the pain at all?

Later I asked Hannah what we should all do.

–Oh that's simple,– she replied. –Every night before you go to sleep you get down on your knees and say "By this time tomorrow fifteen thousand small children will have died." You go on doing this every evening until one day you decide to do something about it.–

* * *

So, by the time you have finished reading this book, in a world of plenty, with waterfalls and blue skies and magic boxes, thousands of children will have starved to death. And if that does not make you angry then you must have had your spirit and your heart surgically removed.

Imagine if the Martians did land now.

Would they see what we see? Would they see people going to football matches and eating Chinese dinners and buying villas in Spain?

No, of course not. They would see people fighting over scraps from the council tip in Thailand or joining the sex industry in Africa.

So we, the poor people of Morocco and the world, publish our manifesto which states, "To all Dictators, to all Leopard Skin Hats, in Africa, Asia or South America, to all crooked and greedy businessmen: a warning. If you keep on taking our money and putting it in your Swiss bank accounts we will take you to the salt mines in the Sahara desert and force you to work there until you STOP thieving and abusing and generally acting like total gobshites."

And I tell you this, it is not difficult. Once one starts, others will follow. Once one African Dictator, one Leopard Skin Hat, one crooked businessman is led to the salt mines then others will follow.

Once one Billy Petersen is warned others will take more care.

Once one *Krap U Luv* is dismantled and sent back to where it belongs and the earth underneath turned once again and fruit trees planted and hens allowed to grub and cluck for seed in the soil, then others will follow.

And of course once one magic box is found others will be unearthed also.

Depose the Leopard Skin Hats. Depose the cruel dictators. Put the greedy nutjobs who make our lives a misery to work on the land.

Because there is enough for everyone! That is the realisation. The simple realisation. If the greedy judges, the evil cases in their horse hair wigs who banged me up for whacking Billy Petersen, took only their share and no more there would be enough left for everyone else.

We cannot continue with one half of the world living on grass and the other half dying of heart attacks because they are too fat.

People rise up! You have nothing left to lose but your Leopard Skin Hats!

Here endeth the lesson.

* * *

In the morning we arrived in the town where Frank had bought the box.

We went into a café and ordered coffee. I put the box on the table and Eric said to the waiter –We are looking for the shop where this was sold.–

I could see by the way he looked at it that the waiter recognised the box.

We went through the medina in the centre of the town, minding the stink and the refuse, following the guide the waiter had hired for us, until we reached a jewellery store on the other side.

The jeweller took the box into the back and I could see him putting a glass to his eye and examining it. Then he came back and shook our hands.

–My name is Ali,– he said. –Please do tell me the story of this box.–

So I did.

And when I had finished and we'd all had a chuckle over the daft things the box had done he said –Now you will go to the house of my uncle, Hassan, who will explain everything to you.–

So we shook hands and then we were outside on the street again. This time we went by taxi to a large house on the edge of town. During the ride we were all silent, thinking that we were finally getting to the heart of the matter.

As we were taken inside and upstairs on to the terrace I said to Leo –This is it mate. This is where we get to the heart of the matter.–

From the terrace we could see over the town to the green of the oasis and the desert beyond.

A servant brought us mint tea and I put the box on the table and then we waited.

After a while I said to Rose –Maybe he's gone for a ride on his camel in the desert.–

–Yeah,– she said. –Or maybe he's in the back pissing himself laughing at the daft foreigners who've come all this way to return a camel bone box they bought in a shop.–

* * *

Finally Hassan came in and I nearly wet myself laughing because he was a dead ringer (Arab version) for Mr Parsons, the English teacher at school who was sacked when the head found him on top of Miss Pond in the staff room.

Smithy the Traveller would have whispered –A pint of Parsons Pond please Albert,– and we would have all burst out laughing.

He even had the same crackly dry voice.

–Good morning to you and welcome to our town,– he said, and I had to duck my face down behind my hand so he would not see me laughing.

Then he said that his nephew Ali had told him about us and that he would be delighted to tell us the story of his brother Mustapha. So we sat back and waited. There was a long pause while he looked out at the view and gathered his thoughts.

Finally he began. –It has been said by some that my brother Mustapha possessed magical powers.–

I looked down at the box.

–And certainly I myself have never met anyone so gifted at managing his camels.–

Further pause to look at the view.

–However it has been said by others that my brother's ability to win continually at dice and cards showed more earthly capabilities.–

I remembered Benny the Jeweller shaking his head over the perfectly cut dice in the box.

–Indeed there were those who unkindly said that my brother Mustapha cut corners in his dealings.–

There was a further long pause while we digested this information.

But then Hassan seemed to cheer up, as if the bad news had all been imparted and we could move on.

–But my brother was also a great adventurer.– He pointed down to a pile of magazines on a side table. –He had plans to travel the world.–

He picked up a magazine and opened it and we saw a picture of the Eiffel Tower. It was indistinct though and could easily have been mistaken for Blackpool Tower. A second photo showed snow scenes from a Northern Country.

I was about to ask Hassan if his brother Mustapha also went to Chinese restaurants when he said –My brother was adventurous in other matters too. When a small Chinese restaurant opened in our town he was one of its first patrons.– I turned to Rose and she rolled her eyes.

There was another long pause and then Hassan said –But the main inspiration in my brother's life was football.–

I sat up in my chair.

–He founded his own club, Mustapha FC. The ground is down there below you.–

We looked down to where a pitch was marked out between two buildings. It was nothing like Athletic. There were just goals at either end and a couple of concrete benches on either side, but it was still a football club.

–Mustapha undertook all the duties. He bought the shirts, marked out the pitch, supervised the training and picked the team. And at night he watched the games from Europe on the television so as to learn the tactics.– Hassan stared at me. I had an idea now of what was coming.

–Then one day we had a visitor. A hot-shot business-man from Casablanca. He told us that there had been a mistake, a legal error. It was he that owned the football ground, not us. And he planned to rip it up to build a hotel.–

Rose touched my arm to steady me.

–Of course Mustapha was like a madman. He said that the hot-shot businessman from Casablanca was a wild dog and that we had no choice but to shoot him dead. It took us a long time to calm my brother down.–

Rose's pressure on my arm grew stronger.

–But then, after a night spent considering it, my brother challenged the hot-shot businessman from Casablanca to a wrestling match, an arm pull, winner takes all.–

He bent his arm sharply at the elbow to show us. –And of course the hot-shot businessman from Casablanca agreed because he knew he would win easily. After all he was twenty years younger than Mustapha.–

I looked down at the pitch. Rose was still holding on to my arm. I knew how the case felt all right.

Then Hassan took a deep breath and said –But against the odds it was my brother Mustapha who won. Because nobody knew how strong he was, especially when he was angry. He let the business-man have the first three pulls, and then he hit him with seven pulls in a row.–

He slapped his hands together suddenly, bang, bang, bang.

I looked around. Everyone's eyes were on me.

–What happened then?– I heard myself ask.

Hassan looked at me carefully.

–The hot-shot businessman went home to Casablanca of course. It was winner takes all and that was that. We were having a celebration up here on this very terrace when the tragedy occurred.–

–When what tragedy occurred?– My voice sounded tinny and distant.

–When my brother slipped on the step behind you.–

We all turned back to look.

–He went down hard. It was an accident of course, something slippery on the floor. But he cracked his skull. Died instantly. Just like that. A terrible shock. The doctor said it was a thousand to one chance.–

We all sat stunned.

Then Hassan gathered himself again and continued. –But my brother, having some foreknowledge of what might happen, had given me his testament the night before.–

That was the moment when it came to me in a flash.

I looked at the box. I wanted to bang my hand on the table and shout that I was right, that Hawking and Einstein and all the rest of them WERE gobshites, but instead I let Hassan finish.

–He told me that he did not want to lie in the desert for a thousand years like everyone else. He said he wanted to travel. He had his plans.–

He touched the pile of brochures with the pictures of the Eiffel Tower and the snow scenes from a Northern Country and then he said –He instructed that his body be cut up and his bones used to make a series of boxes. His son Ali was instructed to make a set of dice for each box.–

By this time he was speaking so slowly we could have all finished his sentence for him. –And the boxes and the dice were to be sold in Ali's jewellery shop.–

Then the door opened and Ali came in carrying a tray with nine identical boxes on it and my box, the last box to be returned, was placed alongside them.

* * *

That night Hassan gave a party for us in the desert.

As we sat round the bonfire looking up at the night sky I said –What about the other people who brought back their boxes? What were they like?–

Hassan stared into the crackling flames and replied –They were just like you Arthur. They all had their stories to tell.–

I looked around and thought of everything that had happened to bring me here to this desert camp. The piggy-eyed doctor, Billy, prison, the escape, Cornwall.

I thought of the slogans that Smithy's Mum had sewn on to the flags:

Those with Benefit Books shall be given Rolls Royces,
And those with Rolls Royces shall be given Benefit Books.

And the Journalists shall become Ratcatchers,
And the Ratcatchers shall become Journalists.

Then I thought of Albert and Albert's Wife and wondered if they would ever settle on a new name for their pub.

Then the Touareg musicians began to play the same rhythmic music Mohammed and I had listened to in prison.

The fire crackled.

The musicians played.

And the talk flowed like wine.

Suddenly there was a terrible shout and we looked up to see Omar the Camel Man running past in front of us and out into the desert night.

Hassan put his head back and roared with laughter.

–What the chuffing hell was all that about?– I asked.

–He was screaming that he has seen the ghost of my brother Mustapha and that he is scared to death!– said Hassan, then he roared with laughter again.

In the middle of the night I woke and went out of the tent to look at the stars. It was still and silent and cold. I felt as if I was back at the beginning of the world.

A group of Hassan's men were curled up in blankets by the embers of the fire. Nobody stirred.

It was then that I saw a silver-grey figure standing a little way off, one foot on a football, looking straight at me. Our eyes met and I knew it was Mustapha, but when I looked again he was gone. After that I went back to the tent and lay down but I didn't sleep.

And when we made our way back into the town the following morning I didn't tell anyone what I had seen.

* * *

As we drove back north to Marrakesh we were all still excited. Even Eric shook his head and said he had never seen anything like it.

Bangkok Rose put her arm around me and hugged me and said –Arthur Polianski you are my hero and I love you. I crown you King of Morocco.–

Then I heard Hannah say to Leo –I admit you may have got a point, but you will not stop me believing in science.–

Only Mohammed was unconvinced. He said –The bloke is a con man. You ask around you're going to find a hundred boxes like that. How big is this guy Mustapha going to be? I tell you the answer to that, exactly the size of a big old camel.–

But as we approached Marrakesh Leo said –I don't know who's right or wrong but as far as I'm concerned the world will never look quite the same again.–

* * *

And so life goes on.

I continue to work with Mohammed making jeans and Rose still works with Hannah in the co-op.

A week ago we sat down with Mohammed and told him that we wanted to double the size of the co-op. We showed him plans for a new building, two storeys high, the top floor comprising a proper schoolroom for the children. Mohammed is considering the idea at the moment.

There are times when we wonder if we have not been rumbled. A stranger appears in Saleem's or there is an awkward glance in a bar or a shop. But then we watch the sun going down over the bay from our roof terrace and we know that everything is going to be alright.

Every so often we get discreet visits from Rose's Mum and Titus, and Titus and Eric have become firm friends.

From time to time we also see Frank and Smithy and Nell and the rest of them. Even Albert was planning to come out, but his wife refused to fly so he had to cancel.

We still argue over the box and what it means and none of us has really changed our position.

And one day we will come home and see everyone.

But not just yet.

FACT

Every year, according to UNICEF, 5.6 million children under five die from malnutrition.
(5.6 million divided by 365 equals 15,342.)

Spain, Morocco, Cornwall, 2005-2007

Printed in the United Kingdom
by Lightning Source UK Ltd.
132178UK00001B/106-123/P